A Father Anthony Savel Mystery

THE GOLDEN FISTULA

John F Toles

For *Cousin*

PROLOGUE

The young, newly consecrated, and overly prissy Bishop sat in his cathedra, the coveted chair of all aspiring priests who desired his position, watched as the plague of the masses came forward to receive the Sacrament of the Body and Blood of Christ on the feast day of the Blessed Virgin Mary. Unlike his civilized and perfected piety, theirs was, at best provincial and at its worse something akin to the trained monkeys he had observed at a local fair that he had viewed from his carriage window. They were always dirty, they were always ignorant, and they were always here, jarring and jostling one another like cattle in a holding pen. When he found it necessary - and it better be for a damn good reason - to walk amongst them, he would insist that they not come within several feet of him and following such an excursion, insisted that his servants burn the shoes and gloves he wore, so as to keep the pestilence at bay.

Losing interest in them for a time - if there had been any interest to begin with - he took to admiring the fine lace of his alb, the white priestly robes, that had been ordered from the city, but the flashes of light that emanated from the amethyst of the obligatory and ostentatious ring on his right hand, which identified him as one of the lords of the Church, kept drawing his eye. If these heathen had any idea who sat in their presence, they would pay him homage, following their reverence to the Savior. Naturally.

He knew full well how he had been appointed Bishop, "they" (the other "they" that sat on red cushions and wore enough gold to outfit all of Solomon's wives) were certainly capable of identifying the true servants of Christ above the clamoring buffoons who strolled through the liturgy as though dancing in a house of whores, but he had no idea how he had found himself in a bishopric of such low regard. My God, the steeple of this cathedral was propped up by several timbers just to keep it from tumbling down on sheep and shit below. He hoped to soon be able to remedy such a foul appointment (enough coins in the right purse always did the trick), but for now, as he was prone to say (and often), this was the cross that he must bear and...

"O my Lord, would you take a look at this one!" he mumbled to himself and the lackey that was assigned to him.

The man in question was past elderly. Bent at the waist, surely only a single degree from the tipping angle, he walked with a stick in one hand - its tip, encrusted with sewer from the streets - and supported on the other side by a daughter or wife, either old enough to have been in the grave for at least a decade themselves.

With disgust on his face, the Bishop unashamedly stared, mouth noticeably agape, as the pair moved forward to receive communion. He could barely stand to see any of them but found himself transfixed by this ancient individual. The young man, in the cattle shoot before them, still covered in the coal he shoveled for most of the day at the local iron smith, received his bread and wine - clearly desiring a large "snort" of the latter - then ducked to the side with only a glance at the Bishop.

Watching, with some premonitory anticipation, the Bishop slowly leaned forward in his chair and observed closely as the old man first received the small piece of bread, the Body of Our Lord Jesus Christ, and the wine, the cup of the Most Precious Blood. Then it happened.

"The fool," the Bishop hissed.

Whether it was the lowly deacon who was serving the chalice or the old man that the Bishop was speaking of was unclear, but as the deacon withdrew the cup from the old man's lips a single drop of wine could be seen by the Bishop, dangling from the chapped blue lips of the old man, like a drop of nectar drawn out from the honeysuckle blossom. Just as the wretched fool reached to wipe it away with his filth encrusted hands, it dropped.

For the Bishop, time slowed. The drop fell as slowly as the shoulder straps of the lace undergarments that the young women wore who came to "receive counsel" late in the evening. Yet instead of eager expectation, the drop produced nothing but pretentious horror.

He moved. Dashing forward like a miscarried arrow from the bow and lunging outward, stretching not only his counterfeit piety, but his quasi atrophied muscles in an attempt to catch the drop of wine from landing on the cold excrement encrusted granite. Had he caught it, the angels would have risen in glorious hymns of praise; as it were, the Bishop came up about four feet short. The sound of the air forced from his lungs as he hit the pavement, masked the soft 'splat' of that most precious drop.

Crawling forward, on hands and knees, tears brimming in his alcohol induced bloodshot eyes, the bishop could only watch as the Most Precious Blood soaked into the grit and stone.

Such a string of profanity had never been heard within the walls of the cathedral, not even when a young apprentice had dropped a load of the same granite pavers onto the architects foot during the cathedral's construction. In his rage, the bishop brought the Mass to a brusque conclusion, even before everyone had received; dispensing with the concluding prayers and - obviously - the pontifical blessing, sending those away who had not received by vulgarly informing them that on this day they were deemed too unworthy and unshriven. He accomplished this while guarding, with his position and ample size, the spot where the drop had fallen.

Following the evacuation of the cathedral, the bishop had the attending clergy rope off the area of pavement and placed candles around the stone to signify its significance and elevate its prominence.

In the days following the incident, the bishop bent his

limited intellectual capacity to the task of devising a plan as to how to remedy the current situation and another to insure that it never occurred again in the future.

The paver was a simple solution: have a stone cutter brought in, washed thoroughly, and then put to the task of removing the paver. Once done, the stone would be cut down to a manageable size and the piece containing the drop of Our Savior's Blood would be placed in a glass ossuary so that it might be brought out on significant occasions and venerated. Granted, anyone desiring to make such a pilgrimage to the sacred stone would be required to make a small offering to assist the elderly man who spilt the Blood shorten his years of purgatory. The paver became known as the Bishop's Stone.

Seeing that the tragedy never occurred again required a bit more thought. Had it been legal, the bishop would have prevented the peasants from receiving communion all together; however, given such dazzling intellect would be lost on the overseeing Cardinal, yet in order to expedite the solution, he had the foresight to turn the matter over to those learned in matters science. The answer of these apple-polishing scholars was revolutionary and something of a scientific breakthrough. It would forever remove such ghastly calamities as the Bishop had experienced on the feast day the Virgin. These educated men, utilizing all their skills and also those of goldsmiths and jewelers fabricated the Golden Fistula.

This most holy straw was approximately fourteen inches in length and a quarter of an inch in diameter. A small circular cup was placed at the end nearest the mouth so that in the event someone was to "dribble," it would be captured and recycled. The bishop insisted that he always be allowed to drink first to avoid any backwash. One of the sniveling deacons could finish what remained at the end of the Mass.

The Bishop was as pleasantly surprised as any, thinking this scientific advancement in the administration of the sacrament would further his cause for a significantly more dignified bishopric. At night, as he lay restless on his fine sheets, he imagined himself not only in a finer diocese, but also wearing red; and on those evenings when he was feeling particularly ambitious - "Lord, I your servant am not worthy!" - white. However, as justice would have it, he never made it. He died from the knife wounds he sustained when the father of a late night "counselee" refused to see "the holiness" in the deflowering of his youngest daughter.

For almost a century, the fistula was the accoutrement to possess, but then passed out of use as the church ultimately decided to withhold the chalice from the people all together, they simply were not worthy. Several fistulas still survive (Pope Paul VI was seen using one in 1964), but many were melted down by the bishops and the gold was put to better use in brothels, breweries, and private residences. Of those that remain, a few are brought out for occasional use, but the majority are buried in the back of bottom drawers of church sacristies across Europe, but not the first. Not the one masterfully created because a bent man had the nerve to allow a dribble, a drop to fall from his chapped blue lips.

The history of the Golden Fistula and the Bishop's Stone (later called the Beggar's Stone in honor of the old man and not a fornicating bishop) passed into legend, but the two items managed to survive and remain united across five centuries, through the end of the Dark Ages, Reformation, Renaissance, Enlightenment, and the empty purses of countless greedy Bishops. As the church made its way across the Atlantic, the two relics would be packed up with other items and sent to the colonies. They would occasionally be transferred from one parish to another, but eventually found their way to a small parish in Milwaukee. Following the bankruptcy of the Diocese due to the detestable actions of several priests and the permissiveness of a few Bishops, the parish was sold and the appointments were disbursed; at which time the Fistula and Stone found their way to The Cathedral of St. John the Evangelist; however, there was no place fitting for such arcane items following the archbishop's 2002 heretical renovations to the cathedral, which transformed a jewel into cheap costume jewelry. Fortunately, instead of sending them the way of the cathedral and as a sign of ecumenical relations, the Golden Fistula and Bishop's Stone were given to The Cathedral Church of St. Matthew's, an Episcopal Church (apostate schismatics - thanks to Henry VIII and his many wives), the denomination that is the rebellious first cousin of the Church of England who have been loving Jesus with a slight air of superiority since 597 a.d., when St. Augustine, the Apostle to the English, was enthroned as the first Archbishop of Canterbury.

The people of St. Matthew's graciously received the items and built a small niche in the sanctuary near the altar to display them, and once a year on the Feast Day of St. Matthew, put the fistula to use, allowing everyone the novelty of receiving communion through a straw (after first explaining to the children that it was not appropriate behavior to blow bubbles). Aside from this annual outing and a weekly dusting, the fistula lay innocently silent and unnoticed atop the paver. Its history, however, was still in the making.

FRIDAY - 2:00 P.M.

The bishop's death had been unexpected, but not unappreciated. Bishop Jeremy Rainer - *"Right Reverend, Sir," if you preferred to remain in his good graces* - had toddled around the diocese for well over two decades, spouting incomprehensible theology, closing churches he deemed too insignificant to spread the Gospel, and stifling every form of ministry that differed from his unpublished and ever changing agenda. When not occupied with these delicate ecclesiastical duties, he would spend a significant amount of his day Googling himself to ascertain whether or not any of his clergy had the audacity to contrive or disperse anything negative about him or his positions in posted sermons, social media outlets, or blog posts. His overinflated ego was matched only by his girth, which was immense. It was always more than a bit ironic - and quite comical - to watch him deliver a passionate sermon on Ash Wednesday on how the faithful should deny themselves when clearly the only thing he denied himself was a second side of corned beef hash with his second serving of biscuits and gravy.

His death was the direct result of his size. The coroner suggested that he did not suffer at all, having expired from a massive coronary before he hit the floor. His office was on the second floor and the receptionist below, when she heard and felt the crash of His Grace, felt certain that either the rapture or the apocalypse was in full swing. She, being the cradle Episcopalian, was uncertain as to which would occur first. The Canon to the Ordinary - *think number two* - a Most Rev. Dr. I've Got a Stick up My Bum Bob Caldwell, upon discovering the toppled bishop, made a heroic attempt at CPR, fearing with each compression that if the "B.P." were to die, he would most certainly be out of a job before Friday, but failed to get even the slightest flicker of life from His Grace, the man who wore more purple than Prince in *Purple Rain*.

The Right Rev.'s funeral was held at St. Matthew's Cathedral in Milwaukee with none other than the heir apparent, the Most Rev. Dean - *his name, not his title* - Harris, Dean - *his title* - officiating. Dean Dean - *Double D to those who cared little for him* - planned the show to the final "Amen" and dismissal, with every torch bearer, acolyte, crucifer, thurifer, choir member, deacon, sub-deacon, *et al* practiced to the point of mutiny. He was rewarded with a perfectly executed liturgical drama, there being only one minor, although potentially personally embarrassing *faux pas*: Double D had forgotten the text of his sermon in his office and had to send a deacon to fetch it. The deacon confessed later, not to Double D, to having taken the long way, checking on her child in the nursery, and managing to sample the cheesecake for the reception before returning, just to make Ol' Double D sweat a bit.

During the reception that followed, the members of the Chapter (those elected lay members of the parish who attempt to see to it that Double D and others don't spend the endowment down so far that there is nothing remaining to repair a leaky roof) spent the time huddled in the corner of the parish hall attempting to determine if there was some shoo-in strategy for getting Ol' Double D, heir apparent, elected as bishop, for there is no better way to get rid of a miserable and entrenched clergy person than to get them elected to an even higher position. Successful or not, they came away smiling, although the President of the Chapter still appeared more tense than usual.

The seventy-eight clergy in attendance from the Diocese, surrounding Dioceses, and the two representatives of the "national" church - *neither of which knew the difference between a lavabo bowl and a spittoon* - spent their time posturing and schmoozing as though they were the frontrunner for the purple shirt and the big ring. Each talking louder than the next and each using more hair product than Donald Trump-and that was only the men.

The other guest of this opulent affair consisted of the upper echelons of the local parish and diocese, in other words, those who could write a hefty check. Those who could not were assigned various roles of servitude made to sound like greater honors, which included pouring wine - *sherry for the more "refined"* - serving finger sandwiches, including the deceased bishop's favorite, sardine, mopping up after the jostled drinks, and sweeping up after crumbly wafers.

It was this latter group that I preferred to remain near. For me, the kitchen is the best place to be during these types of affairs, for it seems that these folks are the faithful. The ones who understand and live out that bit, "The greatest among you will be your servant." They seemed to be the ones who got it without really having to work at it. Perhaps this is why I preferred to be around them, for they had mastered a spirit of humility. I had to work at it with all my heart, for although I wanted to be a saint, I knew that I was not any better than the crowd out there drinking sherry with their pinkies pointing to the seats on the right and left of our Savior. Not only was I not a saint, I was also a curate.

In the great schemes of the church, the curate is a priest apprentice, and it is the tradition in this diocese that anyone graduating from seminary and following their ordination to the priesthood must serve their first three years as a curate in one of the larger parishes of the diocese so that they might learn from the more experienced clergy. *Distinguishing the delicate difference between a 12-year old scotch and a 20-year old scotch is one of the many useful skills I have acquired.* Technically, the curate is the rector (top dog) of a parish who has the responsibility for the cure or care of souls. However, the term has come to mean the assistant (lapdog) to the rector, often assigned the duties that the rector finds disagreeable, which are often the duties that one would think a priest was called for: visiting the sick, giving last rites, caring for the poor, etc. *To be fair, most rectors would probably prefer these duties to the ones they are required to perform, such as raising copious amounts of cash for the upkeep of aging buildings.* So, I am the assistant to the Dean of the Cathedral, a highly prized and prestigious position for those just graduating, and in order to secure it, in my last year of seminary, I was pressing palms and kissing babies as only the best politician can in order to be selected. When I was notified that I had been "awarded" the position, I lit up Facebook with the news - *87 "Likes."* Six months in I found myself wondering if I had made a mistake. Now, fourteen months behind and twenty-two more to go, I find myself dreaming about serving at St. Swytherin's in the Swamp, where the eight faithful congregants serve God with the fervor, peace, and joy as the holiest of those capital "S" Saints. I fear that not only am I a snarky and cynical curate - *who is actually thought kindly of by many* - but that I have morphed into the curate's egg.

In 1895, the cartoonist George du Maurier published in the British weekly *Punch* the cartoon of a young curate sitting at breakfast with his bishop and other fine quests. The bishop remarked to the curate, "I'm afraid you've got a bad egg, Mr Jones." The humble Mr. Jones replies, "Oh, no, my Lord, I assure you that parts of it are excellent!" As though you could have a partially good bad egg. My greatest fear is that I am that egg, thinking that there are parts of me that are good, while knowing the truth: I'm rottin' to the yoke. My 15th century friend and constant companion, Thomas à Kempis, reminds me daily of what I should strive for - *to be an imitator of Christ* - but over these last months I've come to believe that I am walking further in the shadows than ever before, wondering if I will ever discover a way to exorcise the bad parts of the egg and uncover the excellent.

This morning, as I looked in the mirror thinking I should get a bit more sun and combing my somewhat grayed hair forward in an attempt to diminish the receding hairline, I questioned if I had sold my soul to become a priest. Had I become like the Church in Ephesus that the Master condemned in the book of Revelation for forgetting their first love? I had nearly reached a conclusion on the matter, when Mr. Z made his presence known.

Mr. Z was a white standard poodle who was not considered "show quality" by his breeder. Aside from the fact that he is dumber than a bag of hammers, she could not have been any more wrong. When he's been freshly groomed, he's a crowd pleaser, and he knows it. The only problem is that he is so lacking in mental abilities that not only did he fail - *who am I kidding: flunked!* - obedience school, but they gave me a refund and thanked me for being so thoughtful for adopting him.

I was told, prior to his adoption, that the poodle is one of the most intelligent breeds, so I gave him a majestic name when I registered him with the AKC: Ezekiel's Mystical Dream, Zeke for short. After ten years, he still has no idea what his name is, so I've resorted to calling him any number of things in attempts to get his attention, but unless the word "treat" is in the sentence, the result is the same: nothing.

Fortunately, he is not without his gift. The big white fluffy dog can start a conversation with anyone, especially children who have lived in painful situations. I have witnessed a street hardened teen bury his face in Z Boy's neck and through many tears release so much anger and frustration at the world. I've had silent autistic children stroke his silky ears and chatter for an hour or more. He has been the source of many miracles and on the day of the bishop's funeral, he was mine.

He made his presence known with a simple "chuff" as I stood doubting, and I knew he was right: stop staring in the mirror. No one ever said this was going to be easy.

If he was at this reception with me, he would have made it much more enjoyable. Either that or he would have told me to go home, pack the bags, move to Burma, and open a shoe store. It would have been that or return to my job as a high school English teacher that I held after college and before shipping off to seminary. Since neither of those were an option today, when not in the kitchen, I remained as close to the perimeter of the reception as possible, without melting into the walls. Occasionally, I would speak to the few individuals and small clutches of those who were likeminded, though the majority of my time was spent gathering up discarded cups, glasses, soiled linen napkins - *heaven forbid that we should use paper!* - and praying that the entire band of pretentious guests would all suddenly decide to exit. My prayer was not answered.

The last did not leave until near five, leaving the faithful volunteers the job of clearing up the aftermath, working until eight to do it properly and not leave the entire job to Jimmy Owens, the dutiful custodian of the church.

The heir apparent to the cathedra, the bishop's throne, Double D, had made a quiet exit soon after the last of the significant guest had departed. I had seen him turn left down the west cloister - *it was a hallway, but calling it a cloister made it much more grand* - walking in the direction of the sanctuary. He certainly couldn't be expected to help with the chores, and even the faithful believed that. There may no longer be Jew or Greek, slave or free, male or female, but there still remains a caste system in society and it thrives in the church.

When the work was complete and the last of the crew had said their goodnights, I locked up behind them and began my ritual of walking the church, checking doors and turning off lights. Jimmy wasn't scheduled to be in for another day to do the major cleaning prior to Sunday services, and I didn't expect anyone to be in tomorrow, myself included.

The floor plan of St. Matthew's was like many Episcopal churches. It had been added onto numerous times through the tenures of its many rectors. For two of those additions, the architects had taken great care to create a near seamless transition to the original structure, but the last four were as haphazard and confusing as a maze at the state fair. The end result was a labyrinth of hallways and stairwells. A visitor to the church, or even one that had been here several months, could go looking for the nursery where they had left their child and find themselves at the top of the bell tower off the sanctuary. I no longer get lost, but I know that I have yet to discover every hidden nook. Even so, I'm confident enough to navigate the halls with minimal lighting, provided there are no new obstacles that I am unaware of or angry poltergeists waiting to ambush unsuspecting curates.

I opted to first shutdown the computer in my office - *it had originally been a closet* - then made my way through the basement below the office wing to the classrooms. Back on the main floor I went in and wiggled the handle on the toilet in the second stall of the women's bathroom knowing that it would still be running - *it was* - and then made my way down the west cloister.

To the right, before reaching the sanctuary, was the Courtyard of St. Mary the Virgin, perhaps one of the most peaceful places I knew outside of the seminary I had attended. As it was only a bit after eight and I had no other plans, I took that opportunity to visit the Courtyard of Our Lady.

There are days when entering this courtyard must have been similar to walking in the Garden of Eden itself. The enclosed garden, surrounded on all four sides by the building, provided a place of quiet seclusion. The sounds of the surrounding neighborhood were muffled if not silenced, and the spiritual peace that the area provided, silenced all the rest.

At the heart of the courtyard was a statue of the Virgin Mary with six small pews forming a semi-circle around her. She was a traditional form, looking down with her hands outstretched by her side, but her face.... We've no idea what she actually looked like, but our hearts know of her beauty, and the artist who created this work must have had that same understanding of her spiritual beauty and was able to capture and release it here in what was once nothing more than a slab of marble. I lost track of time. As I sat on one of the pews, I remembered how a few minutes before the service of my ordination to the priesthood, Bishop Rainer had brought me into this place and had prayed for me and for himself as we were about to begin this work together. I remembered how he had looked at me with the sincerest love of a father and how with a tear in his eye had embraced me as a son. I remembered how he told me that this work would be difficult, but that it was indeed God's work and He would sustain me. I remembered that he told me that this work could easily taint and harden a person's soul and that we must always guard against that trick of the enemy. I also remembered that he then kissed me on the cheek and smiled.

The encounter lasted only a few minutes, then someone - *I could have smacked them* - called his name from the door and in an instant the facade returned. He was once again Right Reverend, Sir, but for those few beautiful minutes, I saw why God had chosen him as his servant.

I came back from my reminiscences when a raindrop landed on my hand. Turned out it was a tear.

"May his soul and the souls of all the faithful departed rest in peace," I said to myself and to the Virgin and crossed myself. Time to get on with it, Z Boy was expecting me.

FRIDAY - 8:07 P.M.

The original church and sanctuary of St. Matthew's were pure Gothic Revival. With its fan vaulted ceilings, epic stained glass, and a bell tower that stands at fifty-eight feet, the building is truly a gem, especially when compared to the surrounding monoliths of glass and steal. As you enter the church, the first of your senses to peak is that of smell. It is from the residue of frankincense, myrrh - *Heaven* - incense that has permeated both wood and stone. *Not everyone appreciates incense, but when you die, you will smell either it or sulphur. Your call.* The Israelites were required to burn incense in the Tent of Meeting as they wandered in the desert and later in the Temple, thus the clergy of St. Matthew's are expected to do the same. The interior ceilings rise forty-seven feet at the peak and the domed apse above the altar at the east end is designed and lit to provide the worshiper with the very real impression of the transcendence of God.

As I enter, I notice that the Altar Guild (those ladies who with prayerful attention, care for the holy accouterments of the church) have failed to shut off the lights in the chancel, the area in front of the nave with its thirty-three rows of pews, where the choir, altar and bishop's cathedra, the bishop's chair, are situated. It is unusual for them to have forgotten any single detail, and as I make my way forward, tapping the top of each pew with my seminary ring, I remember to give thanks for their service, even if they occasionally must firmly remind me that I am not to touch the brass without wearing the white cotton gloves, which are their trademark of a service well executed.

Having tapped seventeen of the thirty-three pews on the right hand side of the center aisle, I stop. Sitting in the cathedra, which is just to the left of the high altar, is Double D himself. I say sitting, but I mean sleeping. The bishop's ashes have not even settled in the columbarium and here Double D is already taking up residence on the bishop's throne.

"Confidence," I say quietly to myself, then break into a quiet whistle of Maria's song, "I Have Confidence", from *The Sound of Music*, to alert the Dean of my presence. I'm too tired for awkward explanations as to why he is there, so I hope that by giving him notice he will have adequate time to think of something to say other than, "I was trying it on for size." However, as I approach, he does not stir.

Too much sherry, Sir?

"Excuse me, Sir," I call when still ten pews from the front. "Excuse me," I say again as I climb the three steps of the white marble pace, still fifteen feet from him. Nothing. "Sir!"

I then notice the wine spilled on the floor in front of where he is sitting - *you in big trouble.* I stand there in utter disbelief. The dean has been hitting the communion port wine and has passed out cold while sitting in the bishop's cathedra.

I confess that it was one of those rare moments that I wished for a cellphone so that I could have taken a picture of him in all of his liquored glory and posted it to the Book with the caption, "Double D drowns in Dow's." I refrained for fear that he may actually end up properly enthroned in that seat and that I would end up out the door on mine.

Unsure of what to do next, I decided that it best to wake him and take him home where he would have the opportunity to sleep it off in private, all the while praying he would have no memory that I witnessed him in such a state.

I take the last few steps forward, unable to avoid the spilt wine and just as I have reached him...

"Shi..."

The last letter of that profanity in God's holy place was expelled from my lungs in a rush, as I solidly hit the floor, having slipped on the wet highly polished marble.

The knock to the back of the my head grayed me for a

moment. *Did I hear a dog bark further back in the nave?* As I sat up, I felt the back of my head, and drew it away to find it covered in blood.

"That's going to leave a mark," I said with a groan. "Sorry, Sir," I said absently to the Dean, fully expecting my fall to have woken and startled him, but my words fell on less than unconscious ears. "I should be so lucky."

When I rolled over to push myself up, I discovered that I was covered in blood. I knew that scalp wounds bled a lot, but this was ridiculous.

"A fella could bleed out at this rate."

Getting to my feet, I turned again to face the Dean. My heart provided me with a catching pause at the sight. Double D was staring at me, but his eyes were as dead as the rest of him. The wine on the floor was not wine, it was blood, and the blood that I was covered in was not my own, it was his.

I reached toward him to check what my eyes had already confirmed - *having been a priest for less than two years, I was already familiar with the face of death* - but stopped without touching him.

"What...?"

Something gold, a single drop of blood holding to it was protruding from the Dean's chest.

"Dean, sir, what happened?"

It was the prized symbol of ecumenical relations. It was the golden fistula and it had been transformed into a spigot leading into the Dean's chest.

"Dean Harris." This time I knew there would be no response, but I spoke his name for comfort, perhaps even as a prayer.

I heard a door slam at the opposite end of the sanctuary and realized I was not alone. This may or may not be a good thing. Having been at the church long enough, I knew the door was the one leading up from the under-passage. It has a very distinct "bang" as the spring yanks it closed. I do not know what possessed me, but I did not hesitate. Without even calling out,

I sprinted from the altar, taking the three steps with a leap and ran down the center aisle to the south entrance where I had entered. I heard someone running ahead of me, but whoever it was had made it to the far end and turned the corner towards the office entrances, before I caught a look at them. I guessed they were headed toward the south exit and the small staff parking lot out that entrance. So, instead of following directly, I turned left down the hallway that connects the west cloister with the east cloister, between the office complex and Courtyard of St. Mary, heading for the exit from the east cloister that leads to the main parking area.

I didn't plan on catching them, but they couldn't exit the church grounds without passing by me. My plan was to see who it was as they drove by. I hit the crash bar of the door and only then remembered that I had already locked the keyed deadbolt. My head made its second significant impact with a solid object in less than ten minutes.

"Damnit!"

Fishing out my keys I got the lock open. Pushing through, I only caught a glimpse of the taillights as a car fishtailed out onto the main street. I know as much about quantum physics as I know about cars, so I had no idea the make and model, but I committed the pattern of the break lights to memory - *recesses of the gray matter told me I knew who's car it was, but I couldn't place it* - hoping to being able to provide the police with even the narrowest of descriptions.

FRIDAY - 8:29 P.M.

"O God, who hast made thy servant Dean to flourish among the ministers of Apostolic Succession in the honorable office of a priest: grant...."

"Hello! Police!"

"... we beseech thee, that he may also be joined with them in a perpetual fellowship. Through Jesus...."

"Police! Where are you?"

"... Christ our Lord. Amen."

"Why didn't you answer me?" questioned the officer as he came charging up the steps leading to the altar, coming up short when he saw the blood.

"You should bow."

"Sorry. What?"

"Never mind."

The protestant mind may never understand.

"Why didn't you answer... are you hurt?" he asked, finally noticing that I was covered in blood.

"No...well a little, but this isn't my blood," I said, while rubbing the rising goose egg on the back of my head.

"Why didn't you answer when I called?

"I was taking care of Dean Harris."

"Is he still alive? An ambulance is on the way."

"No," I said softly, "He's gone."

"How then were you taking care of him," he asked, as another officer in blue came forward. He bowed. I smiled a little, my faith in humanity not completely obliterated.

Turning to the first officer, I responded, "I was caring for his soul."

"Oh."

"Father, if you wouldn't mind," asked the second officer quietly, "would you please step this way, touching as little as possible? This is clearly a crime scene and we need to maintain the integrity of the evidence."

"Certainly." Dean Harris' eyes were still open and I reached forward to close them.

"Father," he said holding out a hand and patting the air, "later."

"Yes. Of course."

I backed off the marble pace, leaving tracks of blood behind me. For fear of ruining the carpet - *who thinks of things like this at times like this?* - I slipped off my shoes before taking the last step down. Had I known the army of police and crime scene investigators that were to come, I would have gone straight to my office and called the carpet cleaners. The police came and they kept coming. They asked questions and then more. When they came up for air, I found my way to pew seventeen and had a seat. One of the bulbs in a chandelier had burned out and left me somewhat in the shadows.

An hour passed and they still hadn't moved Dean Harris. Looking around to see if perhaps the funeral home had arrived I noticed another figure sitting near the back of the sanctuary on the opposite side of the aisle. He was sitting with his arms crossed on the pew back in front of him with his chin resting on his hands. Perhaps I stared a moment too long, but without moving his head, he caught my eye.

He stood with a slight grimace, bad knees I thought, and began coming my way. As he got closer, I surmised that if he weren't one of the good guys, I was going to be in trouble. Professional football linebacker. Large. Dressed in jeans, plaid shirt, and what looked like a fishing vest. He made his way up the aisle. Perhaps fifty pounds over weight putting him near 295, gray eyes, crewcut, and as I stood, ten inches taller than me. *God, let him be one of the good guys.*

"Mind if I have a seat?" There was no anticipation of

being refused the request.

I took a step, then another and allowed him in the pew. Gesturing for him to sit, we both took a place in the shadows of the sanctuary.

"Detective Thomas Stavlo," he said, reaching out a beefy hand, unfazed by the blood on my hands and clothes.

"Father Anthony Savel."

I leaned back and he leaned forward, assuming the position he had before, resting on the pew in front of us. I felt no need to break the silence and neither did he.

Sitting up straight he turned and asked, "Would you be available to meet with me tomorrow afternoon? I'm guessing your morning just got a helluva lot.... Sorry. A lot busier."

"I'm sure it did, but I've no idea even where to begin. Tomorrow afternoon will be fine."

"Go home, wash the blood off, have a drink, say a prayer, and try to sleep." With that he stood, the gun under the vest was obvious and at the moment, instead of scaring the Hail Mary out of me, it was a great comfort.

I followed him out of the pew. He headed forward toward the altar and I made my way out.

"Padre," he called after a moment.

"Yeah," I answered, stopping and hanging my head but not turning, too scared, too tired to care at being offensive, and not wanting to answer another damn question this evening.

"Is God here?"

I could not think of an appropriate answer, so I started moving again, but as I had reached the end of the aisle, I turned, knelt on one knee and crossed myself. If that didn't answer his question, then nothing would.

The Bishop was dead and the diocese is most certainly in chaos, even without the knowledge that the Dean has been murdered. As I walk across the church yard to the rectory, St. Matthew's being one of the few to maintain a residence for its clergy - *I'm there because it was several steps below Double D's standards*

- I try and decide what I should do. Z Boy is no help with this one, sleeping the sleep of the dead in his chair, so even though it is late, I decide that I must contact the next in charge at the Diocesan Office, which means a call to Canon I've Got a Stick up My Bum. However, before making the call, I fulfill all but one of Detective Stavlo's recommendations. I shower and pour a nice drink, but instead of going to bed, I dig out my Diocesan Directory and make the call.

"Hello." I can smell the scotch and feel the bluster through the phone line, clearly having woken him up. "Canon Bob here."

Canon Bob! Who can take that seriously!

"Hello, Sir. This is Father Anthony. I'm sorry to disturb you." *Drag it out of bed, Buddy, you're about to have earn that paycheck of yours.*

"What is it, Tony?"

Anthony! The name is Anthony. That was my grandfather's name. Tony. This isn't the Sopranos.

"Sir, you need to wake up. Something has happened at the Cathedral."

"I am awake, Tony." As though he knows it is annoying.

"The Dean is dead."

"Yes, Tony. I am very well aware that the Bishop is dead. We just had his funeral this afternoon. Are you drunk," he asked accusingly.

"No, Canon Bob, I am not drunk, and I did not say the 'The Bishop is dead.' I said, 'The Dean - Dean Harris - is dead." There is a considerable silence as what I have said begins to register, followed by a loud bang and a rather audible and profane curse.

"What? The Dean? Dean Harris?"

"Yes." I'm already tired of this man, and I see weeks and months ahead flash before my eyes of having to endure his incompetence and buffoonery.

"Well...."

Well, what?

"Well...."

Deep thought.

"How?"

"Murder."

"Tony, may I suggest you sleep off whatever it is you have been drinking and seriously consider treatment for what is obviously a problem. You know the Diocese will not condone this type of behavior."

"Bob" - *the failure to use his title will just twist him up in fits for weeks, but I hope it will snap him awake and into reality, so I say it again* - "Bob, the Dean of St. Matthew's Cathedral in Milwaukee, Wisconsin, was murdered this evening. I am the one who found him and gave him last rites. The police are still there, and I don't care if the place remains unlocked all night. I have washed his blood from my skin, although I think that it will stain my flesh for years to come, but I thought you would like to know before you read about it in the morning papers. You do read, don't you, Bob?" With that I hung up.

If the idiot wanted any further information, he could Google it. I turned off the ringer on my phone, shut off the light, and prayed.

I woke later that night covered in sweat. The Cross of Christ in the cathedral had been cast down on the altar, breaking large pieces from it. The silver chalice had been cast aside. As I watched, My Lord cried out in fresh agony. I could not sleep. My mind raced as, in those last moments, I wanted to run to the Dean, to save him, to be there when the fear of the shadow of death had crossed his eyes and sank so deeply into his soul. Double D. What an ass I am. He is... was a man of God. So many children and so much fear.

FRIDAY - 10:03 P.M.

After the priest had left, Stavlo moved up closer to the crime scene, taking a seat in the fifth pew and watching the crime scene folks methodically go about their job. They had all witnessed such scenes before - violence, blood, death - but in order to catch the killer, they had to be meticulous in every step. To become lax would mean missing a clue or messing up a piece of evidence that a sharp defense attorney would grab hold of like a hungry grizzly grabs hold of a salmon.

Stavlo was confident in this team of investigators, so after a while, his mind began to wander, taking him back to one of the last times he had been in a church.

"Huh. Must have been thirty years ago," he said, leaning back in the pew.

"Sorry, sir," said an officer who had been standing near by.

"Nothing. Just having a think."

"Yes, sir."

I sure wasn't a "sir" back then, he thought to himself.

His parents had split up about the time that he had learned how not to mess himself. Following the divorce, he had been shuffled around between various family members, but at the age of ten, he eventually settled in with a great aunt, Valencia Stavlo, who saw it more as a duty than an act of love to care for the boy.

"Thomas," she had said, "I've already raised five kids of my own, and I'm not much up for raising a sixth. I'm old and I'm tired, but you are welcome to stay here with me s'long as you mind me, use good manners, and take care of the chores I set you to. Agreed?" she said, sticking out her crooked arthritic hand for a shake.

He gave that a good think before shaking, and she was patient, allowing the boy the time he needed. Finally he nodded and instinctively knowing not to grip to tightly, shook her hand.

"Agreed."

"You can call me Aunty V."

"Yes, ma'am."

"Your room is at the end of the hall on the left."

"Yes, ma'am."

"You're to make your bed everyday and and keep it picked up."

"Yes, ma'am."

"I don't want to have to remind you."

"No, ma'am."

"School starts in two weeks. You will make good grades. Is that all the clothes you've got?"

"Yes, ma'am."

"Well, we'll have to remedy that, won't we? Do you have any Sunday clothes?"

Thomas did not have answer to that one, only an uncomprehending stare.

"For church."

Nothing.

"You do go to church, don't you?"

Thomas suddenly found something interesting about his shoes.

"You are to look at a person when they speak to you. Have you been baptized?"

Looking up at her, he shrugged his shoulders.

"Don't shrug your shoulders. That's what animals do. Have you been baptized?"

"I don't know, ma'am," he said, feeling tears beginning to form in his eyes, afraid that he was already on his way to the next relative.

"Well, then, we'll need to be remedy'n that as well. Go on. Get yourself unpacked. We'll have a little supper here in a spell."

"Yes, ma'am."

He almost ran for fear she would change her mind if he took too much time. He had almost made it to the bedroom when she called to him.

"Thomas."

"Yes, ma'am," his heart skipping a beat as he turned to face her.

"You can call this home."

"Yes, ma'am."

"Do you understand what I'm saying to you?"

He shook his head.

"I hope someday you will," she said, with a thin smile.

He only continued to look at her.

"Go on," she said, "get unpacked, then wash your hands and come help me with supper."

"Yes, ma'am," and he turned and entered the room that would be his very own for the next nine years.

He and Aunty V. had an amiable relationship, he showing her all the respect she had earned and her treating him not so much as boy, but as a young adult who frequently needed advice and the occasional swat to the back of the head (never one hard enough to hurt, only enough to get his attention).

For Thomas, those years were filled with all the joys and pains of growing up. Summer league baseball, fishing, school, an occasional flirt but never a girlfriend, and church. At first, Thomas had no idea how Aunty V. got anything done because she was in church or doing something at the church nearly every day of the week, which also meant that Thomas was too.

Most of the members of Trinity Lutheran Church had more than a few gray hairs, making Thomas the youngest member by several generations, even so, the others were delighted to have him, and Pastor Wade Gooding had taken an immediate interest in seeing to it that Thomas had a solid catechesis.

Within a month of his arrival Thomas was baptized (Aunty V. had gotten him a new shirt just for the occasion) and at fifteen he gave his affirmation of baptism (Aunty V. had gotten him a new suit for that occasion).

Over the years there had been the occasional birthday or Christmas card from one or both of his parents with a few guilt ridden dollars shoved inside, but it wasn't until he was seventeen that he began to once again have any regular contact with them. Thomas could tell from the looks of concern that Aunty V. gave him that she was skeptical, but she never said a word against either parent. The following Christmas, he wished she had.

There was to be a great reunion: mother, father, child. It was to take place at the midnight Christmas Eve service. Shortly after supper, Thomas was already dressed and excited for the time with his parents. When the phone rang at 11:07 that evening, Aunty V. reached over and placed her hand on her well worn Bible. It was all off. In fact, it had all been wishful thinking in the first place.

It was too late for Aunty V. to be getting out, she had attended the early service, so she allowed him to take her car and go.

When he arrived, the lights were streaming out of the stained glass windows and the families were streaming in. He greeted Pastor Gooding at the door and then found a seat midway up the aisle. Only a few minutes before the service began, he noticed a few people glancing over at him, but it was only when one of the mothers came up to him and asked if he would like to sit with their family that he realized he had been crying. He mumbled something in reply, stood, and ran down the aisle, briefly catching the shocked look on Pastor Gooding's face as he passed by. Other than the occasional funeral or wedding, he had not stepped back into a church, and certainly not as a practicing anything. It wasn't that he was angry with God, but being alone and relying on yourself was simply far easier.

The decision not to return to church had brought on the

biggest disagreement he had had with Aunty V. since he had moved into her house; however, she did not argue from a place of anger, only sadness and love, but in the end, she realized that he was now in fact a grown man and capable of making his own decisions. Instead of reproving him any more, she came to him as he was sitting at the kitchen table following the latest round of discussions, and bending over so that she was face-to-face with him, put her hands on his cheeks, and said, "Just remember, you are loved."

"Yes, ma'am," was all he could think to say.

Five months later he graduated from high school with grades good enough to allow him the honor of wearing a few ribbons. That summer was spent working at the local Y and visiting with his few close friends. He was the only one of them headed off to college, the others had enlisted in the service and would be shipping out soon enough. He had wanted to go that route as well, but Aunty V. had encouraged him to do college first and then enter in after graduation if he was still interested. He had taken that advice and years later was glad that he had.

The day he had gone off to college was the only time he had ever seen Aunty V. cry and the last day that he had seen her alive.

"You be a good boy," she had said to him, standing in the driveway next to the packed car.

"Yes, ma'am," he said, as she reached up and hugged his neck. It was all he trusted himself to say, fearing she would hear the tears in his own voice.

At some point during the last nine years, Aunty V.'s house had become home, just as she had hoped it would on that very first day.

Looking toward the ceiling, Stavlo asked, "Are you here?"

"Yes, sir. Right here," said the young officer in blue, stepping up.

"Ah," said Stavlo, standing and stretching his back. "I was thinking of someone else."

"Yes, sir."

SATURDAY - 2:03 P.M.

I eventually fell asleep, but what seemed like only moments later, there came a tapping.

"You've got to be kidding me?"

It was no ordinary visitor tapping on my door. It was one Detective Thomas Stavlo, but at least he bore a gift. No. Not gold, frankincense or myrrh. Something even better. A gift from Columbia. The gift of coffee.

"I thought we were meeting this afternoon?"

"So did I, but if it is later than 2:00 a.m. I'll become a Baptist."

"Try 2:00 p.m. You've had your phone off."

"Good Lord, must I convert?"

"You don't strike me as the hellfire and brimstone type."

For a moment, I had forgotten all about the events of last night, but then it returned with a physical and nauseating rush. I turned quickly and ran to the bathroom, slamming the door behind me. When I returned, if the sounds of my horror had upset him, he didn't hint.

"Ready for coffee?"

"No." I took it anyways.

"Let's chat."

We spent half an hour in the rectory discussing the events in broad strokes. By the time we had finished our coffee, I thought we had reached the end of the interview. We hadn't even begun.

"Ok," Detective Stavlo said, leaning back in his chair, "I'm guessing you'll want a few minutes to get ready."

"Ready? Um. Where are we going?"

"Father Savel, this is a murder investigation. There's more involved than a chat over coffee. Right now, you are not being accused, but you are a suspect. So, to answer your question, we're going over to the church and we're going to walk through all of this down to the smallest detail. When we're done, we'll probably do that again. Sound good?"

That was the quintessential rhetorical question.

"Can you give me about twenty minutes, and I'll need to let the dog out?"

"You get ready and I'll take care of..." He trailed off, looking over at the fur ball who had taken over two-thirds of the couch. *How did he hold it this long?*

"Zeke," I say to his unasked question, "but he won't answer to it."

"What does he answer to?"

"Treat."

At that, idiot boy was off the couch, all wiggles and waggling tail.

"Understood. Go get ready," he said to me and, "Come on you," he said to Z.

Apparently everyone did as Detective Stavlo requested, because without question, I popped off for a quick shower and the Zekester followed so swiftly that you would have thought he hadn't flunked obedience school.

Eighteen minutes later we were walking out the door, leaving the dog for one of his many afternoon naps.

Halfway across the yard, between the rectory and the church (about 100 yards), he stopped and surveyed the grounds.

Although in the heart of the city, the grounds give the illusion of being a country parish, until you looked above the tree line to the surrounding office buildings.

The original plans of the forefathers had included a school and a hospital, so they had purchased a large section of land. Neither of those projects came about, but due to the good stewardship of a sizable endowment, the church had managed to hang onto the land - *unlike so many other churches and institu-*

tions that were forced to sell to survive. The result, a hidden sanctuary in the midst of a modern and ever-expanding city.

"Given its location," the detective said, "this land must be worth a small fortune."

"Rumor has it that we receive a minimum of three offers a month. Each larger than the last."

"Why don't you sell?"

"Why would we? We were here when this city was still a rural village."

That satisfied him.

"Ok," he said, gesturing toward the surrounding grounds, "what's around here?"

"That," I say, pointing towards the south end of the church, is the south parking lot. You'll also hear folks refer to it as staff parking. South of us, over here to the right is the South Woods. Just a short way in you will encounter the Menomonee River, so it won't be developed. To the east is our main parking. Just over the tree line - the Great Hedge - is downtown. The same when you cross over Mt. Vernon Ave to the north and 16th to the west, behind the rectory. Overall, it's about four acres of land."

"Are you the only one that lives on the property?"

"Officially, yes."

"Officially?"

"Being downtown and near several outreach services, there are a number who consider the Great Hedge their home."

"How many?"

"No way of really knowing. We do our best to keep it safe. If something seems out of place or some illegal activity taking place, we do what is necessary to clear it up, including contacting some of your colleagues."

"Alright, how many entrances into the building," he asked, as we start making our way toward the front of the church on the north end.

"I honestly have no idea. Plenty, but most are bolted from the inside."

"Who takes care of the grounds?"

"We hire out most of it, except for some of the flower-beds. Episcopalians are great at certain work, but they prefer to write a check for the manual labor."

"Soft hands."

"But sincere hearts," I responded, a bit bristled. "Episco-palians have a certain elitist attitude, which comes more from their own mythology than actuality."

"Snobs?"

"Romantics. They believe in beauty."

"I thought you were supposed to believe in God?"

Christians who are angry with God are always the more cynical. They have lost one of the virtues: hope.

"This line of trees," I say, pointing towards the line of trees along Menomonee Avenue, "was planted well over a century ago. The small one towards the end is a replacement from twenty or so years back. Lightning took out the original."

"Nice change of subject."

He was one to talk, as I was later to discover.

"The main parking lot," I said as we came around the northeast corner of the church.

He stopped and walked back in the direction we had come.

"What's with the red doors?"

"That's up for debate. Some say a church would paint the doors red when the mortgage was paid, while others think it has to do with the Passover (Moses and the Israelites on their last night in bondage in Egypt) and still others say it is a symbol of the fire of Pentecost and the Holy Spirit. Me? I've read that it goes back to the middle-ages. Then, churches would paint their doors red as a sign of sanctuary. Even a presumed criminal who was being pursued could enter the red doors and not be followed or taken until he had been provided the means for fair treatment. Today, we can enter the red doors and take sanctuary from the evils of the world, spiritual and physical."

"That didn't work out so well for Dean Harris."

"No."

And cursed be the one who did such evil. In the words of my sixth grade science teacher on the day I accidentally set her hair on fire, "May the Lord have mercy on your soul, because I won't." I'm going to need to go to confession sometime soon.

Walking around the southeast corner of the church complex, we entered the staff parking lot. There were two cars this afternoon: Miss Avery's and the Dean's. I wondered who would come for his or if it would stand there for decades as a rusting testament to what had been. Not such a far fetched thought. Episcopalians were not big on change.

"You called this the staff parking lot, but you don't appear to have that many staff."

"No, but as this is technically the Bishop's church, he has parking along with the Dean, secretary, certain chapter members, along with a few part-time volunteer staff like the treasurer."

"Chapter members?"

"Yes. The president and vice-president are the leading lay members of the chapter, the governing body of the church. The vice-president is primarily responsible for the physical plant and the President takes cares of much of the other secular business. They are here quite often, so we provide them easy access parking, plus it is a bit of a perk for serving."

We enter the south entrance off the staff parking.

"To the left are the offices and on to the west cloister, parish hall, and sanctuary. To the right is the east cloister."

"Alright," he said, pulling out a small tablet, "walk me through it."

"Let me just tell Miss. Avery we're here."

"Of course."

We enter the outer office, the realm of Miss. Janis Avery, the seventy-two year old church secretary. The lights were on, but it did not seem as though she were here. As I was about to show Stavlo my closet (aka: Curate's Office) a horrible screaming sob broke from behind us. As we both spun and Miss. Avery came careening out of the Dean's office, threw her arms around me, and between great wails of grief asked, "What... what are we to do, F... F... Fr. Anthony?"

Looking over the weeping woman's head, I said to Stavlo, "Give me a minute here."

He nodded and walked back out of the office.

Miss. Avery had served the last three Deans of St. Matthew's and had worked for Double D. - *She would be horrified - Horrified! - to know that we called him that* - for the nine years he had served here. She knew everyone in the parish - *along with a juicy tidbit of gossip about each* - and everything. Her mind was a Dewey Decimal catalog, with references and cross references, of every occasion that had taken place at the cathedral over the last twenty-seven years.

She was also constantly reminding me of how wonderful the last curate was. I hope to one day reach such a status, but I have yet to turn water into wine and have long since given up any attempt at walking on water.

It took several minutes and a fresh cup of tea to settle her nerves. She had heard the news on the local radio station this morning. I had been so tired last night that I had forgotten to call her, which was inexcusable, so I begged forgiveness until she patted my cheek and sweetly told me how my predecessor would never have forgotten such a thing, but she understood how I could.

Oy.

She informed me that the Diocese had contacted her and that they would be sending someone tomorrow.

"Maybe even Canon Bob," she said with great reverence, "to see to the arrangements for Dean Har...," at which point she broke down into sobbing again.

"I'm sorry, Miss. Avery, I have to get back to the police." As I stood, she jumped up and threw her arms around me once more. After extracting myself from her, I went out and found Detective Stavlo. He was closely examining some of the children's artwork that was being displayed along the walls of the east cloister.

"Sorry about that," I said, walking up to him.

"Not a problem. Maybe we could see that part of the facility later," he suggested. "When it is a bit calmer. Tell me about the evening."

I had no desire to recall those events again, but after gathering myself, I proceeded.

"At the time, I thought I was alone in the church. I'm normally the last one to leave, so I have this routine of going around, checking doors, and shutting off the lights."

"Show me, in the same order as last night."

"Alright. Following the Bishop's funeral, folks began to clear out. When it looked like most everyone was gone, I went to the Parish Hall. This way," I said, gesturing toward the west cloister. "Margaret Simmons was the last of the volunteers to leave. Actually, she's always last. She wants to make certain that they've done a proper job. When I came in she was packing up her casserole dish after giving everything a final once over. I offered to walk her out. This is a relatively safe neighborhood, but you still want to be careful and, well, polite. We went out the east exit, on the far side of the offices."

I walked through these details as we passed through the hallway that is behind the offices and joins the east and west cloister.

"Here," I said, opening the exterior door. "I watched her get to her car and leave. She was the last car in this lot. I then went back indoors, locked the deadbolt with a key..."

"Fire code?"

I pointed to the sign that stated, "This door to remain unlocked at all times while building is occupied."

"Keep going."

"From here, I made my way around to the office and locked the staff entrance."

"No deadbolt," he commented, bending down to inspect.

I waited.

"Continue."

"After shutting off the lights and locking up the offices, I went downstairs and checked on everything."

"Let's take a look."

Making the loop we return to the joining hallway. In the center are the stairs leading down to the classrooms below the offices, consisting of six Sunday school classrooms, the decorations on the walls of each a clear indication of the age group. We make our way through the hall and then ascend the stairwell into the west cloister. An immediate right through an exterior door leads to the Courtyard of St. Mary. Without any explanation needed, I walk into the heavenly aroma and light of this Eden.

"Wow," Stavlo said quietly.

"Yeah. I know."

We take a seat on the bench where I had been sitting last night.

"I come out here when I need a bit of peace. Last night was one of those nights."

"How long were you out here," he asked.

"Honestly, I'm not sure. I stopped to pray."

"Just curious, what were you praying for?"

It took me a second to remember. "The Bishop."

"Likable sort?"

"At times he was. At others... he was human."

Stavlo nodded as though he understood that one well.

While we sat for another moment, it struck me. When I was out here peacefully praying, Dean Harris was just a short distance away dying, maybe even being murdered at that exact moment. If I hadn't stopped here...

"Oh, God."

"Don't even think it," Stavlo said, knowing my thoughts. "You couldn't have changed a thing."

"He hadn't been dead long. I may have could of saved him." Jumping up I almost shouted, "For Christ's sake, I could've prevented it!"

Standing slowly and looking down at me, he responded, "Not at all. Given his wound, I don't think anyone would have been able to save him. Had you come in in the middle of it, you would likely be lying next to him. Sit down," he said, gesturing to the pew. I did.

"I've been in law enforcement for over twenty-five years and in that time I've seen so many things I would like to be able to forget, but they hang on like rabid dogs. In some of the cases I've worked, had we found the culprit sooner, we could have prevented more crimes and saved more lives, but we didn't; however, if I were to dwell on that, then I would likely drive myself off the nearest cliff. If only you had known? You didn't and that fact is not going to change. Don't dwell on it or you'll be asking for directions to that cliff."

He was silent, then stood, and headed for the door.

"Hail Mary, full of grace," I began softly, while staring up at My Lady, "Our Lord is with thee. Blessed art thou among women, and blessed is the fruit of thy womb, Jesus. Holy Mary, Mother of God, pray for us sinners, now and at the hour of our death. Amen."

I stood and turned. Stavlo was still by the door, his head bowed. Hearing me approach, he looked up.

"Ready."

"Yeah."

SATURDAY - 4:21 P.M.

We entered the sanctuary from the west cloister and the wave of nausea from the morning made a lightning appearance. I turned to race back down the hall, but it subsided almost as quickly as it arose.

"You good?"

"Almost."

"Take your time. Walk through it."

I began slowly then let it unfold, relating to him the events of last night at what seemed the same pace they occured. He interrupted only occasionally to clarify certain points, but otherwise was silent, appearing to be visualizing the scene himself as I spoke. I concluded with the two uniformed officers arriving.

"You're certain there was no one in the room when you entered," he asked.

"The lights were out in the nave and only the chancel was lit, but, to my knowledge, I was the only one here."

We climbed the steps to the altar. Dean Harris' body had been removed sometime during the night and the police had allowed the scene to be cleaned earlier in the day. Someone in the church had the wisdom and approved hiring that job out to professionals who had experience in these matters. No sense in subjecting the altar guild or other members to that gruesome task. The blood was gone. The memory was raw and real.

"When you came in and climbed the steps, you saw the blood...."

"I thought it was wine."

"Yes, but when you saw it, did it looked disturbed like

someone else may have stepped in it?"

"I don't think so, but I really wasn't looking for that," I said, trying to recreate the images in my head. "I walked toward the Dean and that's when I slipped."

I laughed.

"What?"

"It's nothing."

"Tell me."

"Well, when I slipped, I thought I heard a dog bark."

"Where?"

"Towards the back," I said, pointing toward the darkened corner of the nave. The light had still not been replaced. "Near the vestibule of the north exit."

"A dog?"

"Yeah."

He was silent, then, "Go on. You slipped…"

"As I was getting up, I realized the wine was blood, but I thought it was mine. I figured I had really busted my head open when I fell, but then I saw the Dean's eyes and realized that he was dead. That it was…."

They don't teach this in seminary. They don't teach how to balance a church budget, how to balance your life, how to fix the boiler, all of which you are expected to know how to do when you arrive in a parish. They also don't teach you how to cope with the murder of your superior.

"That it was the Dean's blood," I manage.

"Then what?"

"That's when I saw something gold protruding from his chest."

"You saw the murder weapon?"

"Yes. The fistula," I said, clarifying.

"Fistula. What is that exactly?" I think he had already Googled it, but I explained.

"Think of it as a holy straw, used to drink the consecrated wine so that no one spills even a single drop."

"Interesting. You touched it," he asked.

"I think so. Yes. It all seems quite surreal at the moment."

"Then what?"

We had been over this, but I answered, "I heard a door slam."

"The one from the hall?"

"Yes. Well, not the one we came in. The under-passage."

"Wait. Not the one back there? The entrance from the west... cloister," he asked, pointing to where we had entered the sanctuary.

"No. On the other side of it. It's next to it leading into the stairwell. Take the stairs up and you end up at the top of the tower. If you go inside that door and close it, you'll see that there is another door and a circular stair case leading down. That door is on a spring so that it will close automatically and makes a very distinctive 'bang,' like the screen door your granma had. Go down and you enter the under-passage."

"Show me."

We walk to the back of the church. To the west of the entrance from the west cloister is a row of paneling, the third panel, nicely camouflaged, is the entrance to the stairwell. Pushing it open, we both enter, a bit like peas attempting to re-enter the pod. Once in, I let the door close without allowing it to slam as it did last night.

"Up leads to the bell tower...."

"Any way out from there?" he asked.

"About a sixty foot jump."

He nods.

"Down," I say, pointing to another small door that is only visible when the panel door is closed, "is the under-passage."

I moved to open it.

"Don't touch that."

Removing a napkin from his pocket, he opens the door we just entered.

"Step out, please."

Z Boy obediently following instructions flashed in my head.

He let the door close softly behind him, but then turned and pushed it open again. He looked up and saw the spring connected to the top of the door and the top of the doorframe. I knew what was going to happen as soon as he did, but still jumped when the door banged shut.

"Did you show this to the police last night?"

"Well, I told them about it."

"But you don't know if they saw it? You didn't actually show them?"

I shook my head.

"Where does it come out?" The frustration that had crept into his voice told me that someone had missed something. I said a quick prayer for that someone.

"In the sacristy," I say, pointing back towards the altar.

"Show me."

"What is the sacristy," he asked, as we walked forward.

It is the most holy realm of the Altar Guild.

"A place where all the sacred vessels, books, and vestments are kept. It is also where the priest and others vest, um, get dressed in the robes, etc. before and after a service."

"I see. And the under-passage, what's its purpose?"

"The clergy and others get vested in the sacristy, so it would be awkward for them to walk down the aisle, only to turn around and come back up for the processional, the opening hymn. They could go outside through the sacristy door, but as I'm sure you are aware, Wisconsin gets cold, so when they built the original church, they included the under-passage. It is practical, not liturgical. Just a way to move back and forth unseen, much like backstage and the undercroft of a performance theater. It's only wide enough for us to walk single file, and it's rather dimly lit, but it serves its purpose. The kids, although they're not allowed down there, like to play in it. It's got a few corners that make great hiding places to scare one another."

I also suspect that the occasional quick make-out session has occurred for some of the older kids.

"I see." As I was unlocking the sacristy door, he asked, "Is it always kept locked?"

"Except when in use. There are many valuables kept here. Also, a safe where the offerings are kept until they can be deposited."

"Who has a key?"

"Clergy, staff, members of the Altar Guild, a few volunteers, and wardens."

"How many keys would you say are out?"

"Twenty or so."

We enter the room and are immediately greeted with a more intense smell of incense, so much having been burned over the decades.

"Please touch as little as possible."

"Right." Gesturing to the left side of the room, "Exterior door, drawers and closets where we keep the various liturgical items, and there is a safe in this cabinet."

I open the door to show him.

"Who has the combination?

"Not sure."

"Do you?"

"They barely trust me to preach without spouting heresy. They're certainly not going to trust me with the cash."

"Continue."

"That opens to the under-passage," I say, pointing to the panel at the far end of the room. Aside from the dark spot on the wood from years of use, you wouldn't know it was there.

He used his napkin and pushed on the spot I had indicated. The door opened in to the left. Pulling out a small flashlight from his fishing vest, he peered in. Even from where I stood, I could see the bloodied hand print on the far wall of the stairwell. He stepped back, allowing the door to close gently, and then stared for a few moments at the closed door.

Turning he asked, "Did you show this to the officers last night?"

"Um, no. I told them about it."

The fact that his blood pressure had just increased even

more was obvious as the red creeped up his neck from under his collar.

"Let's step out of here. I need to make a call."

Halfway through the call he remembered that he was in a church and immediately looked up to see if I had heard his rather colorful tirade. I had. He hung his head. When he looked up again, I gave him the sign of the Cross and mouthed an, "*Ego te absolvo.*" He may not have known what it meant, but he got the gist, gave a humble slight bow, and returned to eviscerating the person on the other end of the line, with considerably less - although not absent - color.

It wasn't hard for me to discern that the officers last night had not understood what I meant when I said "under-passage" and no one bothered to ask. By the time the reports had reached Stavlo, sometime after I had left last night, under-passage had been translated to hall and some very important evidence had been overlooked. Before he ended the call, I knew that the army of police who had been present last night, would soon be returning. I turned and faced the altar as he wrapped up his call. How was this going to end?

"Padre?"

"Yes."

"We need to seal this area off again. Sorry."

"We have services tomorrow morning," I said, turning to face him. "This congregation has been through enough without having to cancel or move them."

"We'll be out by then."

This may be his investigation, but this was God's church and His people. Priorities.

"Afterwards, we'll need someone to tell us if anything is missing from the, um...," he said looking down at his notes, "sacristy."

"I can do that."

"Good. When my people are done, we'll let you know you can go in."

"Fine."

"One last question and then we'll take a break."

"Sure."

"Why did you kill Dean Harris?" His eyes never left mine.

"I'm sorry? What?"

"Why did you kill Dean Harris?" he repeated more slowly.

"I didn't." After a few moments I asked, still a bit shocked, "Am I a suspect?"

"You were until about five seconds ago."

"Well," I said, scratching my head and laughing nervously, "I've never been a murder suspect before."

"If it helps, you weren't much of one."

I laughed again, then turned to the altar and bowed.

"Why do you do that?"

"See that candle up there," I asked, pointing high up and behind the altar.

"Yes."

"When that candle is lit, it means that there is consecrated bread and wine in the tabernacle, that little cabinet just behind the altar. When there is consecrated bread and wine in the tabernacle, then the Presence of God is here in a very real way; therefore, we bow when passing before the presence of Our Lord."

"You did that last night."

"Yes."

"Interesting."

"Holy," I said and turned to leave only to be greeted by the sight of Canon I've Got a Stick up My Bum waddling in from the west cloister, followed closely by Miss. Avery.

"Tony," he bellowed from the back, "I insist on being brought up to speed immediately!"

Looking sideways toward Stavlo, I ask him if he would like to take this one.

"Yeah, no. But I'll make him a suspect if that would help," he says, with a sardonic smile.

"Who is behind this most dreadful deed," demands the Canon as he walks up, puffing from what must soon resolve itself in a myocardial infarction, no less lethal than the former bishop's.

"I'll take you up on that," I say to Stavlo, then turning to Canon Bob, "Let's go to my office where I can explain everything we know."

"Fine, but we'll use the Dean's office. Your closet is too small."

As I walk down the aisle behind the Canon, amazed at his girth, a flash of dread passed through my soul. If he doesn't somehow get his waddling self elected Bishop, what if the Canon decides he wants to become the next Dean? Lord, help us all, I'll renounce my orders and become a security guard in Libya. That seems like a quiet life by comparison.

My thoughts are interrupted by the Canon asking if there is any of the sherry left from yesterday. He must have something for his nerves. My nerves are settling, but I may need a drop or two to keep from becoming a suspect in a second homicide.

SATURDAY - 8:57 P.M.

"Oh, hell."

I had been sitting and trying to change the scenes of last night that kept floating through my head, however, I set the book aside after rereading the same paragraph three times and still uncertain what Sai King was getting at. That's when it struck me. Tomorrow was Sunday.

"Oh, hell."

Tomorrow was Sunday and Double D was dead, leaving me with the service and the sermon.

So much had happened that I hadn't even looked at the readings for this week, and I suspected that even though attendance had wained considerably over the last several years, tomorrow was going to produce a full house. There would be the regulars, and those who dance around the fringes of the church without ever really committing, and then the curious and the morbidly inclined. They would come to see the scene of the crime, closely inspecting the marble to see if they could detect any stain of blood in the grout, although the Altar Guild had assured me that there was no sign of the violence. Then, regardless of who they were or why they were there, following the reading of the Gospel, they would all look to me to speak words of faith and understanding, to be able to bring some sense to the madness of the world.

By 11:00 p.m. I was ready to Google www.hotgod.com, because I had bupkis. How do you explain to the faithful that someone had come into the House of God - *their* House of God - and murdered their priest? It was then I decided to do something different. The bishop would probably be furious, but he was dead. The Canon had left earlier in the day - "*This is just too dreadful. I must allow my soul to retreat.*" *Yeah. Retreat away* - and even though he might hear about it, he would quickly forget. By 11:20 p.m. I was in bed and slept well.

I was right. Sunday morning was Christmas and Easter combined. There were not nearly enough seats to accommodate everyone. The wardens and ushers brought in folding chairs and we sat people up in the choir. Many of the children were seated on the floor, up and down the center aisle and on the chancel steps. Towards the back, I saw Detective Stavlo, leaning up against one of the pillars.

I chose not to vest and wore only a black suit and clerical. As I climbed the pulpit, the quiet murmur became the silence of a sealed tomb. It seemed even the newborn babies were watching and waiting to hear what I would say.

"This morning," I began, "I have nothing for you. We have lost our bishop and our Dean this week and my soul, like your's I'm certain, is shattered. I have no words and nothing I can say will help you make any sense of what has taken place, but God can, and the only place I know to hear His voice is in prayer.

"So, today, instead of a sermon, I invite you to spend this time in prayer. Feel free to leave now or whenever you are ready. You may come and go if you please. I'll be up here if you would like to talk." And then, after a pause and a brief silent prayer, " Let us pray."

With that, I stepped down from the pulpit to the sound of the kneelers in the pews being lowered. The silence continued, the only exceptions being from those who were crying softly and the restlessness of some of the children, but even they seemed to understand that this day was different.

The first person did not get up to leave for over half an hour. I did not recognize them and suspected they were one of the gawkers, even so, I was glad that they had been with us. However, their willingness to be the first began a slow trickle of others. After an hour, half had made their way out, but those who remained did not give a hint that they were even preparing to leave. Some of the younger moms had collected the children and taken them down to the classrooms, so that other parents could continue to pray. I was proud of them all for listening in the silence.

The Chapter President, Mike Leigh, was the first to come forward and speak with me.

"Father," he began - normally it was Anthony with him, but I guess, at least for now, I had taken on a greater roll - "I'm with you. I don't know what to make of all this. I'm so sorry I haven't been here sooner."

"It's OK."

"No, you see, I left town on business right after the bishop's funeral. We had a Saturday conference in Chicago and I didn't know anything had happened until I got home last night. Please know that I wouldn't leave you to deal with all this on your own."

"I know," I assured him again. "We'll get through this, but I'm going to need you and the other chapter members' help these next several months in order to keep this church on track. Your job responsibilities just increased exponentially. They teach you a lot of things in seminary, but this never made it into any of my classes."

"We'll be here, don't you worry."

"Thanks."

Another member was making her way toward me, so he said that we could talk more later in the day.

Turning one more time before he left, he asked, "Do we know when the funeral will be?"

"Not yet. Because of the circumstances, we have to wait on the autopsy to be completed."

"Oh. Sure. That makes sense. Call me," and he was gone, gathering up his wife and two teenage daughters as he went.

To my amazement, it was three hours before the last person left. I stood and watched them go. It was Janine Kline, an attractive single woman and member of the chapter. She dutifully turned and genuflected before leaving the sanctuary. She passed Detective Stavlo as he was coming in. Catching my eye, he held up the Columbian gods' brown nectar. I gave him a smile and waved him forward.

Turning back toward the altar, before he made it up the aisle, I said a short prayer, thanking my Lord for the inspiration for today's "service." It certainly wasn't something I could have come up with on my own.

"I've been to some pentecostal services that were shorter than this," he said, handing me the nectar.

"Honestly, I'm as surprised as you. Episcopalians like to keep things under an hour. You start cutting into tee times and happy hour if you go much longer."

"If that is the case," he said, 'cheersing' me with his coffee, "I might make a good Episc.... Episco.... What?"

"Episcopalian. When you can spell it, we'll baptize you."

Not wasting much time in his investigation, he asked, "Did you notice anyone odd here today or someone acting different than normal?"

"No, but then again, this whole situation is odd and different. This congregation does not consider itself to be the *hoi polloi,* but Episcopalians have always considered themselves to be a bit above the rest. We've descended from Henry VIII - never mind his six wives and rampant adultery - and the Church of England, and for some reason, the mere association with that royalty seems to have gotten in our blood, even if we are descendants of bait shop owners."

Not that there is anything wrong with that! Give me a live minnow and a honey hole and you won't see me for days!

"This congregation most always strikes me as humble, even if on occasion, they have to work at it."

"Interesting," He actually appeared to think so, "but nothing out of the ordinary - aside from the obvious?"

I explained that we would normally celebrate the Mass on a Sunday and that as a priest I may have violated the canons of the church by not doing so, but at the moment, if they wanted, they could have my collar. He understood.

"You've been busy, but have you had the opportunity to go through the sacristy and the rest of the church to see if anything was missing?"

"The Altar Guild could find nothing missing and they'd be the ones to know for certain, but I haven't had the opportunity to verify. I can do it now."

"Let's chat while you do."

We step off the chancel steps and into the north transept where the door to the sacristy is located. Unlocking the sacristy doors and entering, I come up short, staring across to the door leading into the under-passage. Stavlo follows my gaze.

"We got it cleaned up," he says.

"Thanks."

"Find anything below?"

"Nothing of significance."

I make my way to the first of the cabinets and begin looking through them. Checking the Altar Guilds work is a bit like checking Einstein's math: you're not going to find any mistakes. I can't imagine anyone having an interest in the vestments, they are fine, but not something that anyone would want, outside of a church. I open the cabinets that contain the silver: jewel encrusted chalices, pattens, ciboriums, lavabo bowls, aspergillums, etc. It all appears to be here. But then I wonder.

I walk over to the side door that leads from the under-passage. Also nicely hidden in plain sight due to the carpenter's skill, and reach to turn the deadbolt.

"This place is like that video game 'Doom'. There are hidden doorways and stairwells everywhere."

"Yes." That was a comment I could appreciate having loved playing that same game with my cousin many years ago.

I cross the threshold into the altar area, bowing as I cross the plane that divides the high altar and go to a niche on the south side.

I stop, look around and then call back to him, "Have you seen...," I say loudly, unaware that he had followed me across.

I start again, a bit more quietly, "Have you seen the Beggar's Stone?"

"The Beggar's Stone?"

"Yes. A stone about five inches square and two inches thick."

"No. What is it?"

"It is the reason behind the fistula."

"You'll need to explain that one."

I proceed to tell him the myth or legend or facts behind the creation of the fistula.

"The paver or Beggar's Stone," I add, "is the stone on which the drop of wine fell. After the wine dropped, it is said that the bishop huddled himself around the stone until the Mass had ended so that no one would step on the blood of Christ. Then, following the Mass, he had workers remove the stone and cut it down to a manageable size, believing that the blood of Christ was still entombed within."

"Hm. Do you believe that?"

"I've never really found a reason to question it, but I also figure if Jesus can find a way to get into the bread and wine, he could have certainly been able to find a way out of that stone by now."

"That makes sense," he said, "but what about the paver?"

"It was always placed in this niche with the fistula laying across it. Since the beginning, as far as anyone knows, the two have never been separated, but the paver is not here."

"Is it ever moved?"

"Only on the feast day of our patron Saint, St. Matthew. Each year on September 21st we have a great celebration and each person present uses the fistula to receive the wine during communion...."

"Not very sanitary," he interrupts with a grimace.

"Only for those who have received the sign of the beast," I respond. "For those of us who have not, we are granted immunity."

He looks at me as though I have suddenly been transformed into some voodoo priest from south Louisiana.

"It's what we do," I say, in order to move us along.

"Got it," he answers, still looking quite uncertain.

"Anyhow," I continue, "the stone is also presented as a symbol of the enduring presence of Christ. It's a bit too superstitious for some, but in it there is a certain truth for us all."

"And what would that be?"

"I am with you always, even unto the end of the age."

He considers this. "But it's missing? The paver."

"Yes. It should be here. It is not something that even the Altar Guild would move."

He pulls out his notepad.

"Tell me again about how big it is. What color is it?"

"Just a gray stone, five by five and about two inches thick."

"Heavy?"

"Heavier than you would think."

"Anything else," he asks, looking around.

"Not that I can see. This is a very orderly place, very much like the liturgy, everything has a place and time. It all seems in order."

Out of the firmament, "Do you know who killed him?"

Damn. He had a way of catching a fella off guard with the questions.

"No. Honestly, not a clue."

"Do you know if the Dean had any enemies?"

"Have you ever been involved in the church?" I ask, not as a matter of judgment, but in order to help me place my answer in perspective.

"Raised Lutheran."

"Well, I'm not sure about the Lutherans, anyone who would make, much less eat Lutefisk is questionable in my book, but I always tell folks, 'The daytime soap operas and national politics have nothin' on the drama and politics of the church.' You may not have enemies, but with clergy you've got ambition. You've got the purple shirt and the big ring. And with that comes envy and the sin of all sins, pride. Don't get me wrong, Detective Stavlo, the Church is holy, the clergy are serious men and women of God, and the laity in many cases will lay down their lives for Holy Mother Church, but to paraphrase the words of a former Archbishop of Canterbury, the Church is the devil's playground. He is always looking for ways to bring it down and destroy God's people. It's how he thinks he will win and achieve his ultimate goal."

"Which is?"

"The death of God and and the death of hope. Hell may be a place of eternal fire, but what is worse is that hell is a place of complete separation from God. You know no true evil, until you have been separated from Our Father. Then you are eternally lost."

"So the Dean may have had enemies, but worse, he was surrounded by the ambitious?"

"Correct."

"What were they after?"

"The diocese can look outside of itself for their next bishop, but these things are cyclical, so, in this election, in all likelihood, they will look within to find their next bishop. Double D... Dean Harris was the heir apparent."

"If he was out of the picture, then who would be next?"

"Several, but none of them would have been capable of murder to achieve it."

"Padre," he said, closing up his notebook, "when I was just starting out as a detective, I was assigned the murder of a twelve year old boy. Twelve years old. Do you know why he was murdered?"

"No," I said, and I didn't think I wanted to.

"His sneakers."

With that he pulled out his phone and began to make a call. Before hitting "send," he asked, "Do you think you could make me a list of those who might be... interested in the job of bishop?"

"Sure," I answered hesitantly, wondering if he would

think it odd that my name was on the list, along with all the other clergy in the diocese, for the truth to be told, we would all deny any aspiration to the position, but our egos know differently.

TUESDAY - 11:46 A.M.

Mondays are never quiet and yesterday was no exception with one call after another from pushy reporters and a year's worth of prattle from Canon Bob's office. Before lunch I told Miss. Avery to stop answering the phone and proceeded to put mine on "Do Not Disturb," just so that I would not have to listen to the tinnitus-like ringing. There is a chaotic order to the inner workings of any church and we were doing our best to get back to ours.

By mid-afternoon we were both exhausted and a bit shell shocked.

"I just don't know," Miss. Avery said, after coming into my office and before bursting into tears.

If I wasn't the one who was expected to keep it together, I would have joined her.

"Go home," I said, reaching out and taking her hand. "We're both emotionally and physically exhausted, and, believe it or not, we've got another full week of this ahead of us. Would you like for me to call Cassandra in tomorrow for help?"

Cassandra Leigh was Mike's wife. The only one I could think of that could possibly maintain Miss. Avery's standards.

"Lord," she said, rolling her eyes and very much out of character, "that woman could talk Jesus off the cross... Oh, I'm so sorry, Father," she blurted out, before bursting into tears again. "That was so uncharitable."

I couldn't help it. I didn't burst into tears, I burst into laughter, which turned out to be what we both needed.

"Go home, Miss. Avery," I said, when we had regained our composure. "It really is going to be an extraordinary few days ahead and we're both going to need our strength."

Who was I kidding? It would be months before this came close to resembling ordinary.

"You're going to need a bit of rest and so am I. Let's go home," I said, taking her hand again. "We'll get a fresh start tomorrow."

"You'll go as well?"

"Promise you won't tell," I said, grinning.

"Proverbs 11:13!"

"Amen to that."

I would have to look that one up, but from the way she said it, I felt confident my secret would be safe.

Before the day was out, I had received a phone call from Detective Stavlo that the autopsy was completed and Canon Bob's office called shortly afterwards announcing that the funeral for Dean Harris was scheduled for Friday. I was hoping to avoid any duties with regard to the service and was rewarded. Canon Bob took it all, down to the smallest detail.

In truth, it was the diocesan staff that took care of all the arrangements and Canon Bob who took the credit.

It appeared to be Canon Bob's intent to make this as much about him as decorum would allow. After all, what better way to get in front of the electorate of the next Bishop.

In the mean time, I sat down with Detective Stavlo and went over the list of clergy who were RSVPing to the service. For the moment, they were the only ones that could have any motive for the murder. Following Dean Harris, there were five other likely candidates who would have a go at becoming the next bishop. Three men and two women.

"Let's not worry about the men right now," Stavlo said.

"Why's that?"

"Given the size of the handprint, the CSI folks say that it was most likely made by a woman. They're not 100%, but close enough. Who are these two?"

"The diocese has never had a woman bishop, so there is going to be a definite push in this direction, whether qualified or not. First, there is the Rev. Vanessa Hart."

"They don't call her Father, do they?"

"Her? They might. She's fifty pounds overweight - *I have no room to talk* - wears a crewcut shorter than mine, and her facial regime, make-up, etc. is considerably less than all of her male counterparts. But to answer your question, no. Some female clergy actually do go by Father, seeing it as a title with no sexuality attached. Others go by Mother or Reverend."

"Just out of curiosity, what's the rule on calling you reverend or Father?"

"Simple rule - *I think* - Reverend is always written and Father is always spoken."

"Interesting," he says. "Sounds like she has drive, motive, and ability."

I feel confident that she would even give Detective Stavlo a few good rounds.

"The second is the Rev. Heidi Kipling."

With a smirk he asked, "Do you like Kipling?"

"I don't know, I've never kippled before."

"Not as funny as I remembered," he said, shrugging his shoulders. "What do you think of her?"

"Given the opportunity, I'd go to work for her in a heartbeat. Solid theology, excellent administrator, firm but kind. The diocese could use someone like her at the helm."

"Either one of them killers?"

"No," I say without hesitation, shaking my head.

"You said, 'solid theology. Do you think that could have anything to do with this? There is a whole God, religious aspect to this that is out of my department. Could it be that the Dean was murdered for religious matters?"

"I've actually given that some thought. There are a lot of religious nutters out there. That animal that shot up that AME church a while back or the one down in Texas, come to mind. There's always a possibility of that, but Dean Harris was very much a middle of the road kind of theologian. He didn't play it safe, as so many do, but he felt that it was more important to purely present the Gospel message. He would give you social commentary in sidebar conversations and even more over a scotch, but he always believed that the Gospel message was far more radical than anything else. That is perhaps the most valuable lesson I learned from him. So," I said, giving his question a bit more thought, "there will always be acts of violence against the church, it stands opposed to much of what the world sees as correct, but I don't believe that Dean Harris was killed for anything specific to what he has said or done in the past, but there is always the possibility that it could have been one of those random acts of violence against a Christian."

"Perhaps it has something to do with the church, but it could also be random in other ways."

"How so?"

"For starters, there are the 'residents' of your Great Hedge. We're planning to make a pass through there this evening, checking IDs and records."

"If they had something to do with it, I can't imagine that they would stick around. Even so, the church has had a long standing policy to let them be as long as there were no issues."

"Would the murder of the Dean qualify as an issue?"

I had nothing.

"Look, we're not planning on running people off or running them in, unless we have reason to suspect them."

"Be kind."

"Besides," he said, fishing out the phone from his pocket when it started chirping, "since I've ruled you out as a suspect, we've got no other leads other than a bloody handprint on the wall. Give me a minute," he concluded, holding up his phone.

As we had been sitting in my office, I stepped out and visited with Miss. Avery for a moment. She was still fuddled, but the work of preparing for the funeral had kept her busy. She told me that we should expect another full house and the press.

"The press?" I asked, a bit shocked.

"Yes. Apparently the mur... the Dean's death has caught a great deal of attention and speculation. The left are saying it should be expected, because the institution of the church has long since abused the people, blah, blah, blah, and the right is saying that the attack on Christianity is a sign of the end of days, blah, blah, blah."

In any given conversation with Miss. Avery, you were free to fill in the "blah, blah, blah" with whatever nonsense you thought appropriate and you would be correct. She was a woman with little patience for... "blah, blah, blah." As I was looking over some of the preparations, I missed the question she asked.

"I'm sorry, Miss. Avery. What was that?"

She whispered, perhaps fearing that the murderer was near, "Are we safe?"

"Oh, Miss. Avery," I said with all sincerity, "I do believe we are, but I will ask Detective Stavlo to reassure you when...."

"Ask me what?" he said, coming from the direction of my office.

"Ah. Miss. Avery was just asking if we were safe."

"Miss. Avery," he said, pulling up a chair next to her, making full eye contact, "we are never 100% certain on these things, but I believe that you are very safe. What happened here is horrific and scary, but I believe that you are in no danger," he said, reaching out and touching her hand. "In addition, we've increased our patrols around the church, so if anything looks out of the ordinary, we will be on it. You, as always," he said with emphasis, "need to be vigilant in keeping an eye on your surroundings, but you are safe." Handing her one of his business cards, he added, "If you ever don't feel safe, you call me direct on my cell."

She hugged him, blushed, then started to cry again. He sat with her for another five minutes assuring and consoling her.

I stood back, pretending to work, but was actually quite interested in this exchange.

"Let's take a walk to the sanctuary," he said, standing.

"Sure. When we were out of earshot of Miss. Avery I asked him, "Have you ever considered the priesthood?"

"You been hittin' the sacramental wine there, Padre?"

"Nope. Just happen to have an eye for those who might make good deacons or priest. You seem to have certain necessary qualities."

Jimmy Owens was leaving the sanctuary as we walk down the west cloister.

"Hiya, Jimmy," I say, greeting him with a handshake. His hands were firm and calloused from so many years of physical labor.

"Hiya, Father."

"Jimmy, this is Detective Stavlo. Detective, Jimmy Owens."

"Pleased to meet you," they say in unison. Detective Stavlo smiles.

"Jimmy is the custodian for St. Matthew's. Has been for over a decade. Isn't that right Jimmy?"

"Yes, sir. Really wonderful place to work... up until a few days ago," he added, trailing off.

"No. It hasn't been easy," I say, patting him on the shoulder.

I've had this same conversation with so many individuals in the past few days and I still don't know what to say.

"Jimmy, I want to thank you for all the extra work you've had to put in this past week. It really is appreciated. The Dean's funeral is on Friday, so maybe it'll slow down a bit after that. At least for awhile."

"S'why I'm here, Father. Do they's know who kill 'im? The wife is all nervous bout me bein' here."

"Sorry, Jimmy, they haven't figured it out yet, but Detective Stavlo says that we are all safe. Just need to remain watchful."

"Will do, Father. Thank you," he says, as he continues down the cloister.

"Oh, Jimmy," I say, turning.

He pops back around the corner from the joining hallway.

"Yes, Father?"

"When you have a minute, the toilet in the second stall of the women's is still acting up. Could you take another look at it?"

"Sure thing, Father. I'll get right on it," he adds, turning out of site again.

"Thanks," I call out, and to myself, "Good man."

I rejoin Stavlo who had already entered the sanctuary and walked up to the altar.

"I'll need to talk with him. Soon. I know he wasn't here that evening, but he may have noticed something out of the ordinary."

"All I can say is, you better catch the killer before Jimmy finds out who it is. He dearly loved Dean Harris."

"Understood." He continued, "That phone call was from the CSI group with a report from the autopsy. The fistula...."

"Yes."

"...do you recall if it was damaged in any way prior to the murder? Did it have any markings on it?"

"No. It was quite refined. This past year, it was my responsibility to care for it during the celebration. Given its age, it is in remarkable condition."

"So you didn't notice that the mouth end being damaged, as though it had been hammered?"

"No," I said, shaking my head. "Not at all."

"I think it's supposed to be part of your job description, but you're good at keeping confidence. Right?"

"Right," I said, although I wasn't certain that I wanted to hear this.

"Ok. There were a few partial fingerprints on the fistula, but nothing we could work with. However, based on the results of the autopsy and the physical evidence, they were able to determine... here," he says, and grabbing my shoulders, moves me to the center of the chancel in front of the altar.

"Dean Harris was standing about where you are. They believe that the killer was over here," he moves to the niche where the fistula and paver were displayed. "They believe the killer must have picked up both the fistula and something rough and heavy...."

"The paver."

"Yes. Most likely the paver. The killer came towards the Dean with the fistula in her left hand and the paver in the right. When the killer was near enough to Dean Harris, they struck him on the left temple with the paver, causing him to stumble back into that seat...."

"The cathedra."

"Yes, the cathedra. The blow may or may not have rendered him unconscious, but given the position of his body, his age and general physical health, it mostly likely did. The killer... here," he says, repositioning and sitting me in the cathedra, "the killer then placed the tip of the fistula against the Dean's chest and used the paver as a hammer to drive it in." With his left hand on my chest, he made hammering motions with his right fist. The scene unfolded in my mind in such a way that it brought a hellish terror to my soul.

Most gracious, God, bring peace to your servant Dean.

"The fistula entered his heart perfectly."

"I'm sorry?"

"Hmm. Oh... sorry. The fistula entered the Dean's heart at the right depth and location. His heart was like a keg being tapped with the faucet left on. He probably never regained consciousness from the blow to the head and would have, more than likely, been dead within a few minutes from blood loss. The wide dispersion of blood was due to the fact that the heart, instead of pumping the blood through the body, was pumping it out... out here," he said, gesturing toward the white marble. "It was an immensely violent act. Whoever did this, then went back into the sacristy and down the stairs to the under-passage. They would have had a significant amount of blood on them, so to not get any on the panel door, they would have had to turn and push through with their butt. Then, as they passed into the stairwell, they wiped some of it on the wall, leaving the handprint that we saw. There were other blood marks through the under-passage, but the trail ended at the door at the far end," he said, pointing in that direction.

It was obvious, as he described the events, that there was something of a movie reel playing in his mind's eye. He did not take joy in what he saw, but he took joy in his work.

There is a certain type of individual that is able to gaze upon the most hideous of humanity and see beyond the pain of human suffering to the cause of that suffering. It is sad that we need to assign people such tasks, but ever since Cain hit Abel with that rock, we've had the need. Even so, I still can't help but think it effects their souls in such a way that we, as a society, are required to pray for them even more earnestly.

Stavlo stood back and stared, once again visualizing the scene as he had described it and as it may have occurred. As I sat in the cathedra, I continued to pray that the Dean never regained consciousness, in fact, I prayed that he never saw anything of his own death and that he woke to the words, "Well done, good and faithful servant. You have been faithful over a little; I will set you over much. Enter into the joy of your master." I would not wish the events of these horrors on the greatest of sinners.

FRIDAY - 10:00 A.M.

"I am the resurrection and the life, saith the Lord; he that believeth in me, though he were dead, yet shall he live; and whosoever liveth and believeth in me shall never die."

There are many things about the Episcopal Church that some would change, but the liturgy of the *Book of Common Prayer* is a sacred comfort to most. The familiar words and the rhythmic cadence are what draw a broad church into an intimate community of faith. This held true as the service for Dean Harris began.

Over his tenure, as with all clergy, various camps and cliques formed. Those who liked where he was leading the church and those who believed they knew better. Those who thought the sermons were too long and the others who saw them as short and shallow. If he failed to include someone's favorite hymn during the Easter or Christmas service, they may stop giving or not show up for six months in protest. And heaven forbid that he not visit you while you were in the hospital.

It is a common misnomer that priest are clairvoyants, knowing the instant parishioners enter into one crisis or another, and so the parishioners naturally assume there is no need to have them informed, but fly into fits when the priest's psychic abilities prove ineffective.

However, no matter the camp, clique, or protest, Dean Harris was their priest and the love for him was obvious on the day of his funeral, although it would have been nice for them to show such appreciation while he was still among the living.

As Canon Bob began reciting the opening anthem, the

thurifer, then senior Acolyte, bearing the Paschal candle, began the slow procession from the back of the church. These were followed by Dean Harris' oldest son who carried the urn and cremains of his father. The youngest boy held the arm of his mother and the three moved together, taking husband, father, friend to his final resting place.

Canon Bob had placed me in the service after all, as the litanist, and it was an honor to be asked to say the prayers for the man who had so faithfully been my mentor for the past fourteen months. *Today I was wishing that I had been a faithful curate to him.* As I entered the sanctuary in the processional, I saw that it was once again filled to capacity. Some faces were unfamiliar, but most I recognized. The press had arrived, and after a brief discussion, it was agreed that they would be allowed one cameraman - *at the back of the church!* - to record the service and they would then share with the others. It was a comfort to see Detective Stavlo also in the back, standing next to the cameraman.

Following the mass, the Dean's ashes were inunrned in the columbarium, which was across the altar area from the sacristy. He would until the last day, be a part of the church he ministered to for so many years.

When the service concluded, the congregation remained still and quiet as the family was led out, the look of shock still fresh on their faces. Those who served in the altar party followed the family out of the sanctuary in a silent and holy recessional. There was to have been music, but the organist, who had been a friend of the Dean's since his arrival, was finally overcome with grief and could not finish. It would not be held against her. The silence that oppressed was a reminder of the Dean's now-silenced voice.

I followed Canon Bob through the under-passage.

"Flawless," I said to him.

"The Lord is good," he said in honest humility. "Thank you for your service today."

"An honor."

"We'll talk more about this later, but so you know what's

happening, and you can share this with the cathedral chapter," he said, as we entered into the sacristy, "the staff at the Diocesan Office believe that it will be best if we conduct the search for the new bishop prior to looking for a new dean. We intend on providing St. Matthew's all the support we can, but this is new territory for us all. So with a search for a new bishop coming so unexpectedly, you're going to find yourself mostly on your own. Don't fret it, but your curacy may be extended. Right now, you know this parish better than any of the other clergy we have."

"Sir, with all due respect, I've only been out of seminary fourteen months. I hardly qualify...."

He interrupted.

"Anthony, if you had gone straight from college to seminary, I would be more concerned. But you've got a bit of life under your belt. Under these circumstances, that is a valuable asset."

We stare silently at each other, then he reached out and placed his hand on my shoulder.

"Through God's grace, Anthony, you can do this."

I could no longer hold his gaze.

"Yes, Canon."

"It'll be at least twelve months before we have a final list of candidates for bishop, but it may be that one of the applicants for bishop is more suited for dean. We'll have to see who applies; however, some of those that apply for bishop aren't at all interested in anything but the purple shirt."

Unfortunately, they are often rewarded for their efforts and conclude their careers with a substantial salary and a diocese to kill.

"Are you considering placing your name in the hat?"

"Well, I... Jeremy!" he shouted, seeing one of the other rectors standing outside the sacristy, awaiting an audience. "Tony, we'll talk later," he said, with a dismissive wave. Like the chameleon he was, Canon Bob transformed himself almost instantaneously into Canon I've Got a Stick up My Bum. The last sign of honest Canon Bob was when he briefly turned, gave me a sad smile and another firm squeeze on the shoulder.

I took my time unvesting, seeing to it that the acolytes hung up their robes and making sure that all those not staying for the reception were personally thanked for their presence. When I had exhausted all my excuses, I slowly made my way down the west cloister to the reception in the parish hall. It was in full swing.

I was only too pleased to find Stavlo at the back of the room nearest me. He seemed to be watching everything at once. Earlier in the week, it was decided that it wouldn't be necessary, but a wise precaution just the same, to have a certain amount of unobtrusive security, so Stavlo and four other officers in street clothes were situated around the room to keep an eye on the gathering. Stavlo also thought it would be the opportune time for me to point out some of the likely heirs to the throne, although it seemed he had largely dismissed this angle to his investigation.

"You people throw quite a party," he said, as I walked up.

"You should see us when we aren't all collared up," I say with a chuckle. "Heck, I learned to drink scotch and smoke cigars when I was in seminary."

"And I thought cops were bad."

"Speaking of which, all's quiet?"

"The family," he said, pointing to a quieter corner of the room, "is busted up and I'm bit surprised, with all the reverends, fathers, and mothers here, that there isn't anyone over there visiting with them."

So was I.

"Give me a second." I spotted one of my curate cohorts, looking as out of place as any, and asked a quick favor. He said he had seen the family alone, but was unsure, thinking that one of the senior clergy would seek to minister to them. Agreeing that those who weren't politicking for the now open positions of Dean or Bishop wouldn't bother, he quickly made his way to the family.

"Anything suspicious," I asked, walking back over to

Stavlo and the back wall he was holding up.

"Other than the party, you folks are kind of boring. I saw more criminal activity at my kid's kindergarten graduation than I've seen here. At least point out to me the likely heirs," he said with a wave toward the crowd. "I'm pretty sure I've already figured out which one is Vanessa Hart. Over there," he said, nodding in her general direction.

"Oh, yes."

"Based on your description and the number of those bowing and scraping before her, it was pretty obvious."

Had I been drinking my punch, I would have snorted it out through my nose.

"What do you think?"

"If she is the most likely candidate, then we've got nothing."

"You can spot a murderer just by looking at them?"

"No," he said, shaking his head, but not taking his eyes off her. "She seems almost scared. Like she's ready to bolt at a moments notice, but not a guilty scared. A kind of scared like she thinks she might be next."

"Please, Lord," I say, "don't let there be a next."

"Not on my watch."

"Yeah, and Peter said he would never betray Jesus, and you know how that worked out?"

Blank stare.

"You know how that worked out. Right?"

"Yeah, yeah. I told you, raised Lutheran, just can't believe that you all don't trust me on this one. Really, you're safe." That didn't quite work out either. "Where's the Rev. Kipling?"

"Far side. She's always tries to situate herself near a door, allowing for a quick and unobservable exit. I guess it was part of her training," I add with a smirk, "she use to be a Marine."

"Well that explains it and gives her the necessary training."

It takes a moment for what he says to register and when I see him observing her a bit more closely, I recognize my mistake.

"No," I say. "She is not a suspect."

"No?"

"No."

"Suit yourself, but she could probably drown you in that paper cup of punch you're holding."

"I've no doubt, but she would die for you before she would kill you."

"Good enough for me," he said, moving on through the crowd with his eyes.

After a few moments of silence, I spot him. How? There is no way.

"That little...!"

"What," Stavlo looks around quickly. "Oh," he says with a grin.

Reminiscent of Moses parting the Red Sea, Dumb Dumb is parting the crowd, followed by shouts of glee and terror. He spots me and bounds through the room with the happiness that only a dog can know.

"I've no idea how he does it," I say, kneeling down to grab his collar. "The doors are locked. The windows are locked. He can't get...."

"Tony!" Canon Bob is at my side, whispering.

Which somehow manages to come out like a shout.

"This animal is scaring people. Please remove him."

"This animal is my dog and he's too dumb to hurt anyone."

"Irregardless...."

That's not a word.

"... remove him," he says with a hiss and a glare. "This is a dignified gathering."

I so wanted to explain to him how dignified I thought the gathering was, but it must have been obvious as Stavlo firmly grabbed me by the upper arm. Instead of speaking, I grabbed Zeke and we head out.

I let the beast go as soon as we are out of the room. Unless he sees another canine, he'll stick close to me. That's what he wanted in the first place. Separation anxiety.

"Come on you silly poodle," I say, just in case he has a sudden brain fart and decides to go back in.

"You talking to me?" Stavlo, with the wise cracks.

Feeling more than a bit irritated with Canon Bob for referring to Dumb Dumb as an "animal," I only give him an exaggerated eye roll.

"This place is safe," he says, as we make our way outdoors, "but I'll walk over with you. I parked over by your place."

Zeke goes romping across the yard towards the parsonage. He knows home even if he doesn't like spending time there by himself.

"The night of the murder," he says, "you said you saw the tail lights of a car leaving the parking lot."

"Yes."

"Have you seen them since? Or even ones like them?"

"No, but they were familiar."

Why can't I place them?

"Have you seen them here, at the church, before or out somewhere else?"

Having tried so many times to place them does not stop me from trying again, but the answer is still no. I shake my head.

"Alright," he says, as we reach the driveway of the parsonage, "there's something else."

He goes to the passenger door of his car and retrieves something from the seat. He hesitates for a moment, then produces an object in a heavy plastic bag. I know immediately what it is, even though it is mostly hidden behind various labels, the most prominent of which clearly reads in bold black letters and a goldish background, "EVIDENCE."

"You found the Beggar's Stone. Where?" I asked, unwilling and unable to take my eyes from it.

He rolls the bag and stone from one hand to the other. Even enclosed in the bag, I can see the dark stains. Now it was not only the Blood of Jesus that had seeped into the pores.

"Wednesday night," he begins, also looking down at the stone. "We did our questioning of the residence of your Great Hedge. There were six of us coming in from various directions in case someone decided to try and slip away. We found nine individuals in all who appeared to be at least semi-permanent residence. Apparently the south side, near the river is beach front property, as most are at that end. They also say they are less likely to be harassed there as well."

"By who?"

"Mostly other homeless or the occasional pack of youth out for kicks."

"Nice."

He nods.

"Of those nine, one had an outstanding warrant for trespassing, but that was the worst. They all agreed that there were one or two other regulars, but none had seen them or knew their whereabouts. They were all mostly cooperative once they understood that they weren't being hauled in, so by the end of the evening, we did as you asked and let them return to their things."

"Thanks."

He looked at me as though this was not the wisest decision on the part of the church, but it had been an amenable relationship with these residents and no one was ready to disturb it. No room at the inn always crept into the conversation when it was discussed.

"This morning, early," he continued, "back at the office, the investigation team was going over the details. That's when one of the fellas, Riley Koch, saw a picture of the Beggar's Stone that we had pulled from the church website. Next thing you know, he's telling everyone - myself included - to 'shut up and let him think.' We do. 'Boss,' he says, 'I need to go back to the church grounds.' I didn't question, I didn't interrupt his thoughts. I drove.

"We got here about nine, just about the time everyone began arriving for the funeral. Riley looks around for maybe twenty minutes, then whistles me over to the southeast corner of the hedge, and there it was. Pitched in a pile of rocks, like where the gardener might throw them when they turn up in the yard.

"Amazing," I say, almost hypnotized as I listen to his voice and watch the stone pass from hand to hand.

"Truly. When he saw the picture from the website, he knew he had seen it before, but couldn't place it. Then something pinged in his head and he remembered it from the night before, or at least thought he had. It took him those twenty minutes to retrace his steps and thoughts, but...."

He concluded by bouncing the stone lightly in one hand.

"Sounds to me like Detective Koch may have earned a medal."

"Maybe a beer," he said, without even a smile.

"What happens next?"

"Well, you've identified it as the stone we've been looking for, but now it goes to forensics. My guess: those dark stains will prove to be the Dean's blood and," he said, pointing to a spot on the paver through the plastic bag, "you see those small half-moon chips?"

"Yeah."

I already knew.

"I suspect we'll find flecks of gold embedded in them and they'll be the exact circumference of the fistula."

"Then...?"

"Then we go through the residents of the Hedge again."

"You don't really think they would stick around, do you?"

"No, but I also don't know that it would be one of them either. May have been an easy place for someone to ditch the stone. Riley just happened to remember it from all the other rocks in the area because of the shape. It just struck him. Lucky break."

No such thing.

"It could also be one of the current residence who committed the crime, mental illness or something, but then it may also be one of them that hasn't been around for a few days. We're going to have to ask a lot questions, then we start putting the answers together.

"I hope that happens sooner rather than later."

"That's the plan."

"You told Miss Avery that we were safe, but based on what you've said, he…"

"Or she."

"Are there *women* living out there?"

"Four."

Why had I never considered that there would be homeless women living in the Hedge?

"Ok. He or she could be watching us at this very moment."

"Father?"

"Yeah," I answered distracted, looking around the Hedge for a pair of guilty eyes, seeing only shadows and darkness. Even the birds seemed to be absent.

"You're safe."

We weren't.

THE EARLY BIRD GETS...

Miss Avery was one of those rare individuals who was happy in her own skin. There was a time when she thought about getting married like her sister had done, but as time passed, it just seemed like too much of an inconvenience, not to mention, messy. There was also the question of children. She loved every child she ever met, yet she never felt the desire or need to procreate. She wasn't selfish, far from it, or a loner, she simply never felt that her life was incomplete and therefore never felt the need to make any additions to it, except in the area of a cat and baubles. When it came to cats, she firmly believed that a lady should have only one, otherwise the neighbors begin to refer to you as the Crazy Cat Lady. However, when it came to baubles and trinkets, you could never have too many, which is why Miss Avery spent a good bit of her time dusting.

Most every flat surface in her house was covered in kitschy trinkets, the majority of which were of cats and almost all of them were some shade of yellow. It was bright and cheery, but also several layers above gaudy. She didn't care though. It was her house and she loved it. Given her affinity for all things yellow, it stands to reason that she would also own a yellow cat, but Thomas P. was as black as Judas Iscariot's heart, with the exception of a few stray white hairs on his chest and his yellow eyes. It was those yellow eyes that had immediately drawn her to him at the shelter. They, of all her yellow trinkets, were the most perfect yellow she had ever seen, which is why he has been allowed to stay, despite the number of yellow baubles he has knocked to the floor and broken.

"Now I know that I'm leaving early this morning," she said to the cat as he wound his way around her ankles while she prepared his breakfast, "but there has been so much happening this week and I'm behind. My goodness, I still can't believe it... No," she snapped at herself, "I don't have time to cry today."

"Thomas P., you're going to have a long day by yourself, so I would appreciate it if you just behave. No more mischief."

Thomas did not respond.

"I'll be back late this afternoon and we can read this evening after supper. You like that don't you?" She asked, while setting his bowl on the little rug with the cat footprints next to his water dish - with the little yellow fish painted on the inside bottom - and giving him a final scratch behind the ear that he did not object to.

"Besides, you know the bonus of going early," she asked the cat, brushing her dress smooth and checking it for stray cat hairs. "That's right, the traffic won't be so bad. It should be an easy left turn."

Miss Avery had few concerns, but the left turn onto the main street from her neighborhood was a constant worry. For years it had been a 25 m.p.h. zone, but that had all changed when it went to a four lane 45 m.p.h. Autobahn, making the left turn akin to that silly Frogger game the kids use to play. She had written her city councilwoman many times requesting a light be put in, but they only responded by saying that the amount of traffic did not yet warrant it. Clearly they had not ever tried to make a left turn off her street.

"Momma will be back," she said, gathering up her purse and heading out.

Pulling up to the intersection, she bowed her head before looking and said a silent prayer. Then, taking a deep breath, she looked left, she looked right, she looked left.

"Well bless my soul." Not a car in sight.

It was going to be a good day as long as Father Anthony's

silly dog wasn't out as she was trying to get into the church. She loved that dog but was always afraid that he was going to jump up on her and soil her dress or knock her over. As she pulled into the drive of the church, she was delighted to see that the coast was clear. It didn't even appear that Father was up and moving yet. That was OK. The young man worked harder than any of the other curates they had had. Of course, you couldn't tell them that. You had to toughen them up a bit.

Miss Avery knew many things about the church, but the one thing she knew better than most was that parish ministry was not easy, especially for those just starting out. They come out planning to win the world for Christ on their first day, which was wonderful, but when that didn't happen, so many of them were heartbroken or soured on ministry, becoming one of those crotchety old priests that no one wants anything to do with. Best to help ease them into the realities of parish ministry and not let them carry unrealistic notions into their first parish.

Pulling into her parking spot, clearly marked "Miss Avery," which no one had ever dared to take, she shut off the engine, engaged the parking break, and made her way into the building, after checking one more time for stray Thomas P. hairs.

"Well who forgot to turn off the lights," she asked, as she made her way down the hall to the office. "Father Anthony, are you here?"

No answer.

She rounded the corner, stepped into her office and stopped dead.

"Oh, my good...."

The blow to her head was quick and severe. She was unconscious, even before her knees began to buckle.

SATURDAY - 7:03 A.M.

It had been a difficult night to fall asleep. After turning the lights out, I had spent the next half hour playing Jr. Detective, going from window to window, peering out into the darkness, hoping to catch someone - anyone! - in the act of something. The only movement was a small herd of deer, the fawns still in their spots, coming up from the river for some fresh grass. I decided that all was safe when nothing spooked them. Unfortunately, it was one of those nights when no sooner had I resolved one concern, that another would raise its head, even if I had to make something up. However, tonight, I did not have that luxury.

I was still wet under the collar as far as priest are concerned, yet I now had responsibility for the cathedral parish of the Diocese and its flock, because the Bishop was dead and the Dean had been murdered. Canon Bob had said he would be available, but with everything else, I wasn't counting on much. Nothing made sense. Bottom line, I was awake most of the night trying to find answers when I didn't know the questions. If that weren't enough, at 3:23 a.m., Dumb Dumb decided to bark at the wind blowing against the house. Nothing like the obnoxious pontificating of a sixty-one pound furry maniac to jounce you from a fitful rest.

Sleep eventually arrived, but when I woke a little after 7:00 a.m., the thought of coffee and toast - *one of the most delightful smells known to humankind* - sounded far more pleasing than trying to score another half hour in the sack. The coffee and toast were worth it, but there was going to be a wasteland of sand behind my eyelids for the duration.

My prayers and study time were unproductive. The fella who fell asleep and then fell out the window while listening to the Apostle Paul preach kept coming to mind; however, I didn't think there would be anyone to raise me from the dead should I do likewise. Following breakfast, I scrolled through the Book to see what the "friends" were up to, then worked my way through the paper. After fifteen minutes of reading one tragedy after another, I was seriously considering antidepressants, but then I came fully awake when I came across an article on the murder, tucked near the back. It included a statement from Stavlo that he must have given soon after we had visited.

"The investigation is ongoing, but there is no new evidence and we have little to go on. We still expect a break in the case to come and look forward to reporting back soon."

"Yeah. He's not the only one," I said to Zekey Boy, who was now so deep in sleep that it would take much more than my mumblings to wake him. Still, I was surprised that Stavlo had not mentioned the paver.

Jr. Detective arrived again.

"Aha. I see what you did there Detective Stavlo. Not letting the killer know we've found the murder weapon. Very smart. Very smart indeed."

After completing the article, I folded the paper and made a quick run through the morning routine, minus the shave - *the face needs a rest.* I took the Boy out for a short walk and saw that Miss Avery's car was in the staff parking lot and figured she was trying to catch up for Sunday. She wasn't the only one behind. If I didn't produce a sermon for this Sunday, they were going to take my seminary degree away. I almost decided to let her work in peace and I would do the same from home, but then my conscience caught up to me. She may need something. I whistled at Zeke - *he really must be French, because he will spend a considerable amount of time smelling the flowers* - and when he didn't come, which is normal, I walked over and lightly thumped him on the head, in order to get his attention.

"Come on, you. We've got to go to work for a few."

After caring for him for almost ten years, he still didn't know his name, but say something along the lines of, "Let's go for a ride" or "a walk" or "to work," and he turns into an AKC champion of intelligence.

Who really is the dumb one here?

We cross the yard from the parsonage to the staff entrance. When I arrive, Zeke has already been jumping up on the door for several minutes.

"What!" I say, reaching in my pockets for my keys, "Miss Avery won't let you in?"

At the mention of her name, he gives a happy "woof." In his pointy little head, "Miss Avery" is synonymous with "treat." I'm not even convinced that he likes the taste of them, because he inhales them so quickly, but it is a game they play and one I'm fairly certain she enjoys at least as much as he does.

Knowing that she is the only one there, I call out in my usual 'The boss isn't here' Ricky Ricardo manner, "Hi, Honey! I'm home."

No answer. No surprise. She and the boy have their routine and she hardly hears a word I say, until they have completed it. She has no children-other than Thomas P.- and Mr. Z is no substitute, but he's got his poodle ways.

As I walk down the hall, I see Zeke standing just inside the door to the offices, tail down, not moving. Odd.

"What's up, Bud?" I ask, coming up behind him and looking in.

I don't know where I've heard it, probably some movie or maybe Mr. King mentioned it in a book, but scalp wounds bleed a lot. Fine. But when that scalp wound has been inflicted upon a seventy-two year old woman, the archetype of all grandmothers, who is now lying unconscious in a pool of her own blood, then whatever was said in that movie or by Mr. King, goes out the window. What remains is a terror that forms as rapidly as mama can swat a disobedient child. It takes me a few seconds to register what I'm seeing before I move, but when I do, I am as efficient as a skilled surgeon in the operating room.

"Miss Avery?" I call, as I drop to my knees beside her. "Miss Avery."

Nothing.

I can see her chest rising as she breathes, but there is no response from her.

I lean toward her desk, grab the phone and pull it towards me. The cord rakes several yellow ceramic cats onto the floor. I punch the speaker phone button and dial 9-1-1.

"9-1-1 operator," the monotone voice squelches through the speaker. "What is the nature of your emergency?"

"This is Father Anthony at St. Matthew's Episcopal Church," I give her the address. "A member of our staff has been attacked in some way. She is unconscious and bleeding. There's a lot of blood."

"Sir, please hold while I dispatch an ambulance."

"Sure." There is no hold music, but I'm still hearing *Ride of the Valkyries*.

When she's back on the line, I asked, "Can you reach a Detective Thomas Stavlo? He's been working a case here at the church and this has to be related."

"I can get a message through to him," she says in that same colorless voice.

I suppose after hearing calls from the insane to the mundane for so many years, the excitement of others no longer affects you. That said, this is Miss Avery and we should all expect a bit more enthusiasm! A minute later, "I've sent Detective Stavlo a message. Please stay on the line until an officer arrives."

"Yeah. Sure."

Several hours later, I hear sirens in the distance.

"I can hear the sirens, Miss Avery. We'll have you some help real soon."

"How can they get to you?"

"Follow the drive all the way to the back of the church.... hang on," I say, as a second call comes in. Since it is Saturday, we would normally let it go to voicemail, but the caller ID is a number I recognize. It's Stavlo. In the process of switching the call over and still hold Miss Avery's head, I accidentally hang up on the 9-1-1 operator.

"Damnit!"

"Nice greeting there, Padre, we're...," he begins in a cheery voice.

"Miss Avery has been attacked."

It was his turn to swear. *He had a knack for it.*

"I'm on my way. Be there in five. How bad...."

Miss Avery stirs.

"Gotta go!" and randomly hit a button on the phone to disconnect.

"Miss Avery? Miss Avery, can you hear me?" I ask gently, leaning close in to her.

She groans softly, then says, "I thought we were safe."

I must not have hung up, because from the speaker on the phone there is another swear, followed by a well-timed expletive.

"Thomas," Miss Avery declares in a soft, but scolding voice.

"I'm sorry," he says repentantly. "I'm so sorry, Janis," but this time he was not thinking of his language.

I'm a bit shocked at that. I so rarely think of Miss Avery as anyone other than Miss Avery, but he reached passed her position and spoke to her as a person. *I am a selfish priest.*

"It's OK, Thomas," she said weakly, before looking up at me and saying, "You are a good man. Am I OK?"

"You're banged up, but you're OK."

They must have turned off the sirens as they drove through the parking lot, because the next thing I hear is the staff door banging open and then the hellhound poodle losing his mind.

"Oh, that damn dog!"

"Anthony!"

"Sorry Miss Avery." I'm now the penitent one. Then, yelling in Dumb Dumb's direction, "Zeke, you miserable beast, let them in for cryin' out loud!"

He did, but then came and stood solidly between Miss Avery and the office door. When the EMTs arrived in the doorway and tried to come closer, he did not bark, but instead let out a growl that even made me nervous.

"Zekey Boy!" Miss Avery scolded, but Zekey Boy was unrepentant and unmoving.

"Ok, buddy," I say softly, and slowly reach over and take him by the collar. "Let's give these nice folks some room to work."

Dumb? Maybe. Loyal. He could be a member of the Pontifical Swiss Guard.

"Come on you silly rabbit," I say, walking him back to my office. He wouldn't appreciate being locked in that closet, but it would have to do for now.

Returning to the front office, I watch as the police secure the scene and the EMTs attend to Miss Avery. They were bringing in the gurney when Stavlo arrived.

"Son of a...," he began when seeing Miss Avery in such condition.

"Language, Mr. Stavlo!" she squawked softly. "You boys are both asking to have your mouthes washed out with soap," she said, gently smiling up at us both.

"Sorry," we said in unison.

We quietly watched as they placed bandages around her head and then loaded her on the gurney to be transported to the hospital. The elderly and knocks to the head do not mix well. Even I knew this. At a minimum she would require an MRI and observation for a few days.

I looked up at Stavlo.

"Damnit," he whispered, fearing that Miss Avery would hear him even though she had already been wheeled from the room.

It was a mess, but we had quite a few more clues. Miss Avery's and the Dean's office had both been ransacked. I hadn't seen the rest of the offices, but I was guessing that it was going to take a while to sift through the aftermath.

"We're going to need Jimmy," I said to the room.

"Not until we've had a chance...," he was cut off when a uniformed officer came barging breathless into the room.

"Where's the med crew? We've got another victim downstairs."

We didn't speak, we just started running. In one of the classrooms downstairs, in the middle of a pool of water from an overturned mop bucket, sat Jimmy. The goose egg on his right temple looking angry and rising quickly.

SATURDAY - 9:07 A.M.

"I'm not going to be able to forgive myself for this one," Stavlo said, as we watched the second ambulance with Jimmy on board pull away.

"God will," I say - *thinking maybe I would too... eventually.* "Can we go back in or do we need to wait?"

"Couple of hours. They're going to need to go through the scene and collect whatever evidence they can find." After looking back over the room from the doorway, he added, "Maybe more than a couple."

"I need to get the boy."

"Riley?" Stavlo barks.

"Yes, sir," a younger man responds, quickly stepping out of the Dean's office.

"Open the first door on the left," he says pointing, and adds almost too late, "and step back."

Z came bounding out, stopping only briefly where Miss Avery had been lying before heading toward the staff parking lot exit.

"Got time for some coffee? My place," I say, opening the door and giving the animal his freedom, something I was deeply envious of at the moment.

"Yeah. It's my day off, so I spend it working."

"Know that one," I say.

We cross the yard to the parsonage in silence, watching Z run from one entertaining scent to the next.

"He likes wine," I say, approaching the house.

"Who?"

"Dumb Dumb. But it makes him sneeze."

"I thought it was bad for dogs?"

"He's French."

"That actually explains a lot."

We return to the silence as I go about making a pot of coffee. It must be all things French, because I'm a fan of the French press when I have time to drink a pot.

I come in with two mugs and find him staring at the bookcases.

"*Keats's Poetry and Prose. The Anti-Nicene Father. The Godfather. Harry Potter. The Practice of the Presence of God.* And enough Stephen King to choke a horse. Padre," he says with a snort, "your bookcase may explode from pure contradiction."

"You'd be surprised. If you can't preach the Gospel message using Harry Potter as an illustration, then you're a lightweight when it comes to hermeneutics."

"And Stephen King?"

"Stephen King is a lot more spiritual than I think he even realizes" *or will admit.*

With another of his abrupt changes in conversation, he asks, "Other than shock and horror, what was your immediate impression when you walked into the office?"

"Surprised," I say, after a few moments thought. "Not the surprise that you get at a surprise birthday party or anything like that. More, 'what the heck,' kind of surprise. It's not like we're hiding state secrets in there. We freely share everything, mainly the Gospel. If we were the headquarters for the Umbrella Corporation or the equivalent, I might be able to understand, but we've really got nothing to hide."

"Is the church wealthy?"

"As far as most churches go, probably yes. We have an endowment of a little over six million...."

"Wow. Seriously?"

"Yes. We've been here for well over a hundred years and people give money in large gifts that they place in trust with us to insure that we are here for another hundred years. I always wonder at how much good work we could be doing with it, but it is legally tied up. Whether I like it or not, it will insure the church remains financially healthy."

"Does anyone have direct access to those funds? Could someone be embezzling?"

That is not something I had even considered, but being the curate, I am not that close to that aspect of the church's business. We discuss it at the chapter meeting, and the finance gurus show up once a quarter to give a report. There's never been anything exciting discussed.

"It may seem odd for some churches, but it is fairly standard for larger Episcopal churches to have substantial endowments, but embezzling is not something I've considered."

"Who handles all the other funds?"

"Well," I say, considering the options, "there are the ushers who count it after the service, the pledge clerks who make the deposits, and the treasurer."

"Can you give me the names," he asks, pulling out his pad.

"Yeah," thinking how paranoid you become after several incidents. I give him the names, including Hank Slidell, the Treasurer.

"Who has access to the funds once they are deposited."

"They are pretty tied up at that point. It takes two signatures to write a check and approved minutes from a vestry meeting, plus two signatures to withdraw from the endowment. I suppose you could probably easily pull it off, but we're not talking millions here."

"Other than the endowment?"

"Yeah. Other than the endowment. So if a thousand goes missing here or there, someone really will take notice."

"What about a hundred here or there?"

I've no idea, but I'm saved by the bell. After checking the caller ID, I say, "I should take this."

He nods.

"Hello."

"Fr. Anthony, what in the world is going on?" Mike Leigh's tone is accusatory enough to imply that I am directly responsible for what has taken place.

"Hey, Mike." *Mike Leigh*, I mouth to Stavlo. "I wish I knew. Just really scary right now."

"How are they?" You can hear the terror in his voice.

"By the time they were taken away by ambulance..."

"Ambulance!"

"Yeah, it wasn't good." A chill runs through me as I remember seeing Miss Avery. That could have gone so differently. "But they both were conscious and talking to me before they left."

"Jimmy's a tough one, but Miss Avery... Miss Avery."

I can tell he has nothing to contribute at this point, only calling to check in and confirm what he has already heard through the church grapevine - *which is extensive* - even though I have no idea who could have started the flow of information - *a.k.a. gossip.*

"I'll be down in a few minutes."

"Mike, that's OK," I say quickly and shaking my head. "They won't even let us in the building at the moment. I'm at my place going over a few details with Detective Stavlo." The last thing I want is a keyed up chapter president bouncing around the place.

"Fine," he says, to my consternation, "I'll meet you there." And with no opportunity to rebut, he hangs up.

"We're going to have company," I say to Stavlo, while glaring at Zekey Boy.

I quickly busy myself in hiding a few dirty clothes and dishes before the chapter president can arrive to discover that his curate has a certain unkempt lifestyle. Funny in that it made no difference to me when Stavlo walked in.

"I thought you people were on this? I thought you said we were safe," Mike demanded of Detective Stavlo as he came in the front door, with not even a hint of a greeting.

Six-four and two hundred ninety-five pounds can move quicker than you think, and Stavlo was on his feet before Mike was no more than two steps in the door. Mike wasn't small, but he was more round than tall. He stopped, then took a small step backwards. Detective Stavlo had a certain intimidating persona that quickly reminded the room who was going to be in charge. Even Zeke managed to be quiet and stand still for a moment.

"Mike," I say, just to let everyone know that I was still present, "take it easy. We're going to work this out."

Still looking uncertainly at Stavlo, he says, "But Miss Avery," and adds as an afterthought, "and Jimmy."

"I know. They're going to be OK," I add calmly, Stavlo already taking his seat once again, surely realizing that Mike was no more a threat than Z, who had already found his chair. "Have a seat," I say to Mike. "Let me get you some coffee."

"Got anything interesting to put in it," he ask.

"Just a bit of my cousin, Glen," I say, with a sideways glance.

"Just a touch, but don't tell the wife," he adds with a humorless wink.

Mike has been the regional manager for a string of dollar stores for more than two years and keeps looking for the promotion that may or may not come. He works hard, but there is something about him that says he does not work quite hard enough. The profit margin in retail is small and Mike always seems to give the impression that he is eating those last few pennies, rather than earning them. That said, he is a brilliant chapter president and from all appearances, a devout Christian. I wonder if the others thought the same of Judas Iscariot?

"Mike. Is it OK if I call you Mike," Stavlo ask. *He's good.*

"Yea. Sure."

"Who killed the Dean?"

Even Zekey seems to perk up at that one.

He is silent for longer than I would have anticipated, then hangs his head.

"I don't know. I really don't know." A tear runs down his cheek.

"Mike," I say, moving towards him. He waves me off.

"I'm sorry. This really has been too much. These are people I love and care for. The Dean. Miss Avery. Jimmy, for crying out loud! What the hell did he ever do other than clean up the," a wave of the hand, "around the toilets? I honestly don't know who would be capable of all this." He wipes his hand and looks to Stavlo and then to me. "Are there any new clues?"

"We'll know after the CSI folks have a chance to work the scene."

"Shouldn't you be over there," he ask, still looking somewhat defiantly at Stavlo.

"Could be, but over time I've discovered, at this stage in the investigation, I just get in their way. Things make more sense to me when no one else is around."

I began to think I was right about it all playing through his head. All the pieces become a series of pictures, melding into a movie. I say a brief prayer that there was a way to delete those Bram Stoker home movies.

Stavlo's cell phone rings.

"Yeah.... hang on." Taking the phone from his ear, he asks Mike and I, "Would the safe have been unlocked? Would there have been anything in it?"

"Yes," Mike says and explains the procedure. "It would have been unlocked. The week's offerings are picked up and deposited on Thursday or before. It is left unlocked until after the late service on Sunday mornings, so that the offerings can be secured. If there was anything in it, it would not have been much."

"That would normally be true," I say, correcting Mike, "but it should have been locked. The offering from the Bishop's funeral was substantial. It was collected for his pet project: Emerging Artists' Consortium. If it wasn't locked, then that would have been an oversight or they had already collected it and prepared the deposit. We can ask, but I doubt that happened," I say, looking to Mike for confirmation.

"Bottom line," Stavlo asked.

"It would have been locked," Mike said, nodding his head in agreement.

"But, we'll check."

Mike nods again to confirm.

Stavlo's eye roll was audible.

"Yeah, but we'll need to verify," he says, speaking again to the person on the phone. "Ok. How much longer? Thanks," he says after a brief pause. "We can go over after lunch," he says, to Mike and I.

"Oh," Mike says, "I've got to get home. I've been gone a lot recently, work, you know, and the wife is not pleased."

"I meant to ask: we got so busy with everything," I say with a wave of the hand, "how was your conference?"

"Huh? Oh, yeah. Went well," he said absently as he rose and headed for the door. "Doesn't look like they'll be promoting anyone from the region this year. Maybe next time."

Zeke trots over to see what's up. Mike reaches down and scrubs him on the back.

"Did the twins take their ACTs yet," I ask, as I walk him to the door.

"Next Saturday. Trying to keep them focused, but teenagers... my goodness, I don't think I was ever so busy when I was in school. I don't like them being plugged into their smartphones so much, but honestly I don't know how they could manage their schedules otherwise. I'd forget my birthday if I were them."

That makes us both laugh.

"We're going to figure this out."

Stavlo had snuck up behind us both as we were walking to the door and we both jumped when he spoke.

"What's that," Mike asked, turning quickly.

"I want you to know," he said, reaching out to shake hands with Mike. "We're going to figure this out and catch whoever is behind it all."

Mike had a soft heart and so Stavlo's sincerity and kindness caught him off guard.

Quickly wiping his eyes, Mike said, "I've no doubt, but sooner rather than later is preferable. And for God sake," he said, placing a hand on my shoulder, "don't let anything happen to this one. We need him."

Too damn many emotions these days I think, looking down for fear that my own emotions would give me away.

"No," Stavlo said, without hesitation. "This one we keep safe. This one has other things to do."

The three of us stood there in silence for a few, almost prayerful moments until Z spotted a yellow Lab trotting freely through his realm and lost his....

SUNDAY - 1:18 P.M.

Attendance was still up at the regular Sunday service; however, this time it seemed I knew everyone, only that everyone was there. A bonus for them all was that I was actually able to figure out something to say for a sermon, having fallen back on Dean Harris' example, and preached the Gospel.

Between the services, the Sunday School went well, and it was then that I noticed Stavlo wandering the halls, although he did not attend either service or Sunday School. I gave him a wave from a distance, but Sundays, surprisingly enough, are difficult days for visiting. *Never tell a priest anything in passing on a Sunday and expect him or her to remember it come Monday morning.* Stavlo seemed to understand this without being told. He left some time after the second service had begun.

Following all the activities, I stuck around and made sure the place was locked up, which seemed to be high on everyone's agenda today, including Mike's, who followed up behind me checking all the doors. *I was following up the chapter person of the day's check. A small case of good old-fashioned paranoia had set in with us all.* Giving everyone a final send off, I would see Mike again tomorrow evening for an "emergency" chapter meeting, and I was certain that Stavlo would be around, I headed out for a few pastoral calls. Number one on the list was Miss Avery, then Jimmy. They were both still at St. Anthony's Hospital downtown.

Sunday traffic was, as always, at a minimum - *no great crowds headed to church* - and I made good time. St. Anthony's was one of the few hospitals that still had clergy parking near the entrance, but today I thought a good stretch of the legs was in order, so I parked at the far end of the lot.

As I walked through the parking lot and entered into an area of more cars, I encountered a woman coming from the hospital. I made to go around her, but she altered her course to have an encounter. *The dog collar could be a magnet.*

Not today, please, I thought to myself. I'm really just too tired.

She said nothing, but instead, extended her arms in a gesture that said, "Hug." I smiled and responded. She hugged me and I hugged her. Afterwards, she took a small step back, then reached out and placed her hand on my face.

With tears in her eyes, she said, "Thank you."

I tried to respond, but found myself also a bit choked up. I nodded and smiled. She went about her business, but when I turned, she was gone. *"Do not neglect to show hospitality to strangers, for by doing that some have entertained angels without knowing it."*

After asking at the desk, I found my way up to Miss Avery's room, 726. I knocked gently, and when there was no answer, entered quietly. The lights were off, the curtains were pulled, and Miss Avery was snoring softly. I do not recall being as thankful in that moment as I had been in a long time. It wasn't that I didn't want to visit with her, but the opportunity for peace was overwhelming.

Fortunately, hospitals have learned that there are some who will be present for as long as is necessary and that the hard plastic chair was not suitable for such circumstances; therefore, they had begun to place at least one "lounging" chair in each room.

Keeping the vinyl squeak to a minimum, I took a seat. I watched for a moment to make sure that I had not woken Miss Avery... Janis, then leaned back, staring at the ceiling. I tried to pray for Miss Avery, the church, Jimmy, anyone, but my thoughts kept drifting back to the prior afternoon as Stavlo and I made our way through the offices and lower level classrooms, after the CSI team had completed their work.

"Let's go take a look."

"I'd rather not," I said, standing, despite my apprehension. "Give me a sec. Need to let the boy out." I had a feeling this "look" was going to take awhile.

"No problem."

I let Zekey out and watched him trot off to his favorite "men's room."

"You know, Lord," I said, following Z at distance, "it would be good to be a dog and have the world as your toilet. Well, I don't mean it like that! You know what I mean," I said giving Him a nod. I was beginning to feel a bit too much like that seed that fell along the path. Then again, it had been so many days since I had prayed, that it should be no surprise that I was feeling disconnected.

"This is just a bit too much," I continued. "Violence. Murder. Death. Do you understand?"

OK, idiot boy. Exactly who do you think you are talking to?

But tonight, it seemed like I was talking only to myself. I gave Z a few more minutes of sniffing about, then called him.

"Come on, buddy. Work to do."

He stopped, but the tone of my voice must have given it away. The dumb one knew that he was about to be left alone again.

"I'll give you a treat. How would that be?" I said, hoping my pleas and look of anguish would generate enough sympathy from him to save me the extra steps needed to collar him, but apparently my acting was not good enough. Walking over I gave him a good tug, which finally started him moving towards the parsonage. Even so, he managed several side trips before making his way indoors. Once inside, he hopped up onto his chair and with a heavy sigh, gave me a sour look, then curled up with his back to the room.

"Well, he's in a mood," Stavlo said, with a smirk.

"He's French."

"Maybe he needs a touch of wine," he said, heading out

the door.

"Maybe I need a touch of wine and a little less violence."

"These days, Padre, you're the proverbial drop of honey."

"Yeah, well," I say, turning to lock the door, "Start swatting! This needs to stop."

We walked across the lawn to the church, both likely considering what we would find upon entering. I wasn't shaking, but when it came to unlocking the doors, I hesitated.

"Let me, probably best anyways."

"Sure," I say, handing him the keys.

Everything appeared in order until we reached the office doorway. From there on, it looked like an Oklahoma tornado had passed through.

"The CSI crew has done their job," he said, "but if you see anything out of the ordinary... I mean, other than the obvious, don't touch it. We can't fingerprint everything."

"Sure."

He walked in, but I stopped at the door. The pool of Miss Avery's blood was more than I cared to see, but there was also something evil present that I could not see, which had not left the building with the person who had committed these crimes.

"You OK, padre?" He asked, looking back.

"No."

He nodded, but then, turning to his work, he returned his attention to the room, taking a big mental picture at everything before examining the details too closely. I could see the movie beginning to develop in his head.

Why did I need to be here? I knew how to handle the things behind the veil, but these up front brutal actions were not my area of expertise.

"How do you look at this on a regular basis without losing all faith in humanity," I asked, still standing in the doorway.

Continuing to deliberately move around the room, he started speaking as though he were alone.

"I've done this a lot over the years. Thankfully it's not someone I know, at least in most cases," he said, nodding toward the pool of Miss Avery's blood. "I kinda flip a switch and turn off my emotions. I start to look at things clinically. I catalog one item at a time, making sure not to hurry or miss anything. You never know what little bit of information will help you to later catch a killer. A shoe print, a cigarette butt, all of it can give you the information you need to convict someone. But, regardless of how clinical you are, the picture still remains in your head. You push it down, and drive on. The bad thing is how it pops back into your mind at the oddest times, and when it does, its a bit like a greasy pizza popping back up into your throat. I was working an accident scene once, not too far from here actually, along the interstate. A young kid got ejected and face planted in the median. The trunk of the car was full of drugs, and it was obvious he hadn't been alone, but everyone else had managed to scatter before we arrived. To this day, every time I drive past that spot, I can see that kid's face, dead in the median; and every time I see his face, I wonder who loved him and didn't have him anymore. I wonder about those who so callously abandoned him to save their own butts. I wonder...," he trailed off.

The evil hovered gleefully in the room.

"What do you see," he asked suddenly, startling me from my own thoughts.

I stare at him, the question, "What do you think I see?" written across my face.

"No," he says. "What do you see, other than the obvious, that isn't right?"

Other than the obvious? He must be referring to the blood soaked carpet or the shambles that the rooms were left in.

"I don't know," I say, after looking from room to room for at least fifteen minutes.

"Look again."

I shouldn't be a priest, because in my head I just gave him a sailor's worth and from the look on his face, it may not have all been in my head.

"Try again."

"Ok," deep breath, "It seems to me that someone was looking for something."

That was so obvious that I feel like an idiot as soon as the words cross my lips.

"Good. What are they looking for?" he asked, without judgment.

"Honestly, I don't know. What the hell could we have in here that anyone would be interested in?" My anger boiled over - again. "For crying out loud, we're a *church*. We are in the business of Jesus and the Gospel! It looks like these assholes are more interested in the money than they are the church!"

"Bingo," he says, softly.

"What?"

"You've seen what I thought was obvious, but not everyone would. You wouldn't think a church had this many financial records, but it seems that's what has been rifled through the most." He looked at me for confirmation.

"Hang on," I say, holding up my hand and walk towards the treasurer's closet - *larger than mine* - and look in. Stavlo is close on my heels. "This...," gesturing toward the room, "everything seems to have been gone through in here. Everything."

"What did you notice about the Dean's office?"

"That just seemed to be his personal notes. I've got a dozen posty notes going at any one time and a 'To Do' list with the larger projects. I picked up both of these practices from the Dean. In his office it seemed they were more interested in... I don't know... his thoughts and projects, than they were anything else. In here it's all about the financial records."

"You must not have anything of interest," he said, nodding toward my office.

Not so much as a pencil out of place.

He let it go.

"If the Dean had something he was working on that he didn't want prying eyes looking at...?" he asked, looking around the wrecked Treasurer's office.

It came to me.

"This is so cliche that I'm embarrassed to say it."

Stavlo spares me by saying it himself as we walk back towards the Dean's office.

"Little black book."

"Little black book," I said, turning to him.

"Where would he have kept it?"

"Coat pocket. Always."

"We catalogued the evidence," he said, rubbing the top of his head, "and there was no black book. Anywhere else he may have kept it?"

"Home, but I doubt it. He always had it with him. It looked like this," I said, pulling one from my pocket. "It is the quick thought. Maybe a note to remember to do something, a sermon idea, or other 'to do'. Probably wouldn't make much sense to anyone else, except the one who wrote the note."

I held it out to him. He moved as though to take it, then dropped his hand.

"It's OK. I've got my own variety of a little black book. Mostly it's private."

"True."

We spent another half hour looking over things, but nothing more surfaced. Downstairs produced even less. Jimmy had been hit hard, the doctors said perhaps even harder than Miss Avery, but unlike Miss Avery, Jimmy wasn't cut. Without knowing what actually happened, someone would think that he had only tipped the mop bucket and slipped by accident, knocking his head on the floor. Whatever had been used to hit him and Miss Avery with was not found.

My reminiscences of the day before were interrupted by prayer. My prayer was interrupted by sleep.

I didn't know how long I slept, but when I woke, the light in the room was much dimmer, and sitting with Miss Avery, holding her hand and talking softly was Detective Thomas Stavlo. I didn't want to be accused of eavesdropping, so I made the appropriate waking noises. They both turned to me smiling.

More accurately, she smiled and he smirked.

"Got your snore on, I see," he said.

"How long was I out?" I asked Miss Avery, doing my best to ignore him.

"The nurse came in and gave me my medication about 1:30," she said softly, but with much more strength in her voice than she had had the night before. "It's almost five now."

"Holy....!"

"Language, Fr. Anthony!" Stavlo said in his best Miss Avery impression, which even got her to smile and give him a playful swat.

"You needed the rest," she said in a gentle voice. "He wanted to wake you, but I wouldn't allow it."

"I appreciate that, but we have chapter tomorrow night and I don't even have an agenda prepared."

"Oh, my goodness!" she jumped, with a hand to her mouth. "Who will take minutes?"

For all twenty-seven years that Miss Avery has been the secretary of St. Matthew's, she has only missed a chapter meeting and the taking of minutes once and that was to attend to her sister who had been quite ill, *and it should be noted, recovered fully following our Miss Avery's visit.*

"Don't you worry," I said standing, "I'll ask Miss Kline. She has volunteered to help you out in the past."

"I know," the tears were on the verge, "but still...."

"Rest," Stavlo said, also standing and reaching out and lightly gripping her shoulder. "It will be OK this time."

"I suppose you're right, dear," she said smiling and reached up to pat his hand.

What the...?

"I'm sorry, Miss Avery, I've been zero company to you, but I need to run. I want to stop by and see Jimmy, he's on the floor below...."

Her face dropped and it was clear that she had no idea Jimmy was here also. Stavlo's look and rolling eyes declared in no uncertain terms that I was an idiot.

"What," she asked, in horror. "Jimmy? What's wrong?"

Stavlo explained that he had an accident, but that he was going to be fine. "Accident" was a rather loose term being used to describe how someone had intentionally forced a rather substantial object to collide with Jimmy's head.

When her blood pressure had decreased a few points and we had prayed, I again made an effort to head for the door. No sense in being the bearer of any more pieces of happiness.

"You know," he said, as we walked toward the elevator together, "that was some pretty good pastoral care back there." He could not contain his chuckles.

"Yes, yes. Open mouth, insert foot. How long were you there anyways?"

"Half an hour."

"She OK?"

"I hope to be that sharp at her age. Most likely the scotch'll kill too many brain cells, though."

"Truly an adult beverage," I say, hitting the down button at the elevator.

"Mind if I join you for this?"

"Not at all, but I've really only got a minute. By now, Z Boy's probably got to go to the mens' so bad that he's sitting at home with his legs crossed, and I've got a lot to do before chapter tomorrow."

"Church leaders. Right?"

"Right."

We make our way to Jimmy's room and are greeted by the shrill accusatory voice of his wife, Nancy.

"I thought you said they was safe!" she all but shouted as she marched across the room towards the door we were entering.

I stopped, Stavlo did not and it only took that small action to gain control of the situation. She was still hostile, but she moved back to where she had been at Jimmy's side, with the bed between her and Stavlo.

A nurse popped her head in. "Everything Ok?" she asked.

"Fine," snapped Nancy.

The way the nurse ducked out made it obvious that they had had more than a few run ins with her.

Taking my eyes from her, I looked down at Jimmy. I knew what I was seeing, even though I didn't know the name of it. A suction and drain had been surgically attached to his head in order to drain the blood and fluid that had been gathering around his brain, causing pressure and other complications. He was awake, but heavily sedated.

"Hey, Fr. A.," he said weakly. "Sorry about all this."

"What are you sorry...," Nancy started, glaring at me.

"Hush," he said softly, without looking at her. "I'll be back on my feet soon. Get everything right as rain."

"Jimmy," I said, drawing close to him, "Jimmy, don't worry. If it stacks up for weeks around there, we'll be fine. It's about time more than just you did a bit of work around the place."

"Thanks, Father," he said, smiling and seeming to feel appreciated. I hope he knew how much he was.

"Jimmy," Stavlo asked quietly from behind me, "did you see or hear anyone?"

Jimmy looked blankly around me toward Detective Stavlo.

"You remember Detective Thomas Stavlo, don't you Jimmy?"

"Oh, yeah," he said, after a moment, recognition crossing his face. "You fellas need t'figure this out."

"I agree," he said with a nod of the head. "Did you see anything?"

"I was mopping the floor in classroom three," he said, looking off as though replaying the events, "and I remember - Lord you'll like this one Rev. - I think I saw an angel."

"Dang fool," Nancy said angrily. "Ain't no such thing."

He looked over at her and then back to Stavlo.

"There was what I believe was an angel, then... well,

then, I woke up downstairs in the emergency room. Father," he said, turning to me, "do you believe in angels?"

Holy Michael, the Archangel, defend us in battle. Be our safe-guard against the wickedness and snares of the devil....

"Yes, Jimmy. I do."

"Well, then," he said, looking over sternly at his wife before turning back to me, "there was one in the church yesterd'y night."

"Jimmy, I believe there was more than one. You're going to be OK and Miss Avery, upstairs, is also going to be OK. The angels are, indeed, watching over us."

"Amen and amen," he said.

"Amen," Stavlo added.

Nancy only glared.

MONDAY - 8:42 A.M.

With Miss Avery and Jimmy both out, the volunteers descended on the church like only Episcopalians can, and once they got past the horror of Miss Avery's blood pooled on the floor, they went to work. By mid-morning, those who did not have day jobs formed a small army: cleaning, sorting, organizing and filing, while others kept everyone caffeined and sugared up. At noon, lunch was ordered. *Chicken Caesar Salads and sparkling water. How could you go wrong?* Miss Avery called about half way through the meal with a good report on herself and had even been down to see Jimmy, who she said was looking "frightful," with the tube coming out of his head, but was definitely improving. That one call transformed the cleaning party into a raucous festive occasion, so gathering up my laptop, I made my way to the Courtyard in order to get some work done before the chapter meeting this evening.

By mid-afternoon I had everything in place and began sorting through items in the office that the volunteers were unsure about. As I sorted, I kept looking for a clue as-to why all of this had happened, but nothing stood out. I asked around if anyone had seen Dean Harris' black book and although they all knew what I was referring to, they had not come across it.

"Would you like me to contact, Sharon (the Dean's widow) and see if she has seen it," asked Cassandra Leigh.

"No. The police have already asked, and I can't see upsetting her over it. It'll turn up," I said, while thinking that if the murderer took it, it was already ashes somewhere. "Could you tell if all the financial records were there? Was there anything missing?"

"None that we could tell, but we've not been able to do much more than get it all in piles. It'll take a while to sort that mess out and probably only Hank will be able to determine if anything is missing."

Hank Slidell was one of the best treasurers the church had had for many years. He had gone through at least a decade of old files, put everything onto the computers and consolidated a good many accounts. In truth, the church really had no idea what it had until he had completed the task. In his final report, he demonstrated to the chapter that there was a little over $200,000 unaccounted for, but given the poor record keeping of the past, it was no surprise to anyone. With a combined sigh of resignation, the chapter opted to write it off and move forward, establishing and using better business practices. I hadn't thought of that $200,000 until then.

"Thanks, Cassandra," I said, walking back to my closet and closing the door.

I considered it for another few minutes, then dialed the number.

"Stavlo," he barked on the other end.

"Do you think $200,000 is enough a motive for what is going on here?"

"I'll be there in ten minutes."

He made it in eight.

"What do you mean, is $200,000 enough of a motive? I told you before, I've seen folks murdered over a pair of kicks," he said, sounding a bit exasperated at the fact that it had taken so long for me to bring this up.

"Kicks?"

"Yeah. Kicks. Sneakers. Why don't you tell me about the $200,000," he said, taking the other chair in my closet and pushing the door closed with his foot.

"I really don't have all the details, and the chapter was wrapping up all the business on it about the time that I started." I paused, trying to get what I knew, which wasn't much, straight in my head.

"In the church, if you do something once, it is an event. If you do it twice, it is a tradition. Try and change it and everybody shouts in perfect pitch harmony, 'But we've always done it this way!' I had a buddy almost lose his job for not including *Silent Night* during Christmas Eve Mass."

"Seems minor."

"It is minor, but when the largest giver of the church brings their three month old first grandchild to Christmas Eve Mass, just so that the child can hear *Silent Night* for the very first time and it is not sung, well you as a priest have joined the ranks of those progressive heretics that want to use guitars during the service."

"Dealing with folks like that, I'm beginning to wonder if Dean Harris might not have offed himself." With a wave of the hand, indicating we should move on, he said, "Tell me about the $200,000."

"Tradition. It goes back to tradition. Within the archives, you will find all the records of the church, the chapter meetings, and the finances going back some 150 years, and all of them are hand written. I think it was part of the job description that you had to have exceptional penmanship to be the secretary or treasurer, because they truly are something to behold. It wasn't until 1981 that they started using a ballpoint pen!"

"Oh for pity sake," he said.

"Yeah, and from the sound of things, the treasurer resembled Ebenezer Scrooge hunched over his books." I discovered that I was speaking in a low voice, afraid that I would be overheard disparaging the practices of the church. "Anyhow, over the last twenty years, the church has been in a slow decline; therefore, the talent pool has shrunk. When the old treasurer retired, they had a difficult time finding someone new. Hank said he would take the job, but only if they were willing to give up their pre-Reformation methods of keeping the books. He wanted a descent computer that would allow him to set up a proper finance system for what anyone would consider a small corporation."

"So they hired him," he asked, leaning forward.

"No."

"No?" Leaning back, again.

"They held out for six months, still trying to find someone to keep up the 'old ways,' but when Dean Harris opened a few pieces of mail that had been gathering and discovered that the power was soon to be cut off because of lack of payment, he made an executive decision and hired Hank. The chapter gave him grief, but when he explained how difficult it was going to be to worship in the dark, they grudgingly agreed."

"How long has he been the treasurer?" he asked, leaning forward again.

"He started a few weeks after me. About fourteen months."

"What's he like?"

"Nice enough. I was always a bit surprised by the amount of time he spent up here initially, but he is single, so I figured he was like a lot of other single folks, just killin' time."

"Killin' time, huh?" he said, leaning back again.

"Look, there's no reason to accuse him. He's well liked in the church and the community."

"Tell me the rest," he said.

"Within a couple of days of being hired, he was given the closet across the way there. A new computer showed up a day later and then he was on board, working late into the evenings getting things square. Can you believe that he discovered we owned a hundred acres in Montana that no one knew about?"

"If you all ran the place like you say, then I'm not surprised. Go on."

"It's funny. You come out of seminary and the folks that hire you think you have all this knowledge on how to run a business, but when it comes to that aspect of managing a church, most priest are idiots."

"For crying out loud," he said, throwing up his hands, "take a course in business!"

"I did. Several."

"Good on you. What happened then?"

"He would keep us paid up on all the current bills, but his primary concern was confirming the history, and his main focus was the past ten years. The chapter decided that anything before that was already a wash, so Hank went through the years and when he had a year completed, he produced the necessary reports showing the chapter the results. There were a number of mistakes found, primarily addition and subtraction errors, with a few others that he referred to as 'common accounting errors' when doing this kind of work by hand."

"So how did those 'common accounting errors' add up to $200,000? I've got to tell you, if I make a $200,000 addition mistake, my bank is going to let me know about it."

"Well, you have to understand, they keep several accounts. There's the checking account where the day-to-day business is taken care of: salaries, utilities, etc. A good bit of money moves through that account, but the larger money moves through the investment accounts. That's where the millions are located, most of which can't be touched, except for the earnings."

"You know why so many folks think the church is a racket, don't you," he asked, raising his eyebrows.

"Never crossed my mind," I say, then cross myself, which elicits a bark of laughter.

"Anyhow," he says, again waving his hand.

"Anyhow, by the time he's all said and done, the church is less $200,000 on its balance sheet. The chapter is a bit stunned...."

"How many of granma's pension checks do you think that adds up to, burning up in the plate," he asked, skeptically.

"Granma's got oil wells in Oklahoma if that's where it came from," but going on, I continue, "they're stunned, but they also want to move on. No one wants to spend too much time trying to figure out who was responsible for such a significant loss, because even accountants that make such grave errors are pillars of the church. He told them there was a $200,000 addition error and they believed it."

No sooner have the words come out of my mouth, then I realize my tone. - *"Do not judge, so that you may not be judged."* - I have convicted Hank Slidell. Stavlo has not.

"It may be that he's just a good accountant," he says.

And I am a bad priest playing at being Joe Friday.

"Yes. He really is. He's a partner at one of the major accounting firms downtown."

Stavlo stares up at the ceiling for a moment before speaking.

"He's got means, talent, and motive, but is he a killer?"

I don't answer that one.

"I'll need to talk to him."

"If he is innocent, I would like for him to remain our treasurer. Try not to scare him," I say, adding, "church treasurers are almost as hard to come by as church organists."

"I would think you could go out to the local ballpark to hire an organist," he said with that smirk of his.

I stare. He moves on.

"Ok. There's one other item we need to discuss," he says, pulling out his pad. "Simon Presley."

"That's not a name I'm familiar with."

"How about Elvis or the King?"

"Presley?"

"Simon Presley, a.k.a Elvis or the King is a resident of the Hedge, or he was up until a few nights ago. Disappeared about the same time the Dean was murdered."

Those words are still a shock to the system, but I immediately know who he is referring to, even though I didn't know his name.

"I know him."

"How?"

"Elvis. He sort of carries himself with that Elvis swagger and in an odd sort of way, he dresses like the original."

"Ever interact with him?"

"Only in passing. He came in on occasion asking for a bit

of cash. Never anything large. He was never polite, but not rude either. Callous."

"When's the last time...."

"Last week." *Damnit.* "The Dean had gone for the day and Miss Avery and I thought we were alone in the building - *I'd completely forgotten* - he walked in the office and startled us both."

"What did he want?"

"Usual. Just a few bucks. Didn't say why."

"Do you know where he might be if not here?"

"No idea. Some are more transient than others. You see them around for a few days, then maybe not for several weeks. I'm sure you know...."

"Yeah." He was impatient. "Ever any trouble?"

"None that I'm aware of."

"We've got to find him. Some of the other residents said he normally camped near wear the paver was found. He's got a record," he said, checking his notes. "Mostly minor stuff, but perhaps escalating. Most recently a trespassing and possession charge."

"He could be in Buffalo by now."

"No. He's around and...."

He was interrupted by a knock on my closet door.

"You in there, Father," Mike Leigh calls. "We're about to get started."

"Oh, hell," I say quietly - *I may have said a few other things* - looking down at my watch. "Chapter time."

Stavlo may have said, "Language, Father!"

MONDAY - 7:06 P.M.

"... and bring us all to be of one heart and mind within your holy Church; through Jesus Christ our Lord."

"Amen," the chapter concluded in unison, their assent to the opening prayer. I thought it best to open with something from the Book of Common Prayer rather than my own ramblings.

I had anticipated Mike leading the meeting, but when I looked to him, he and all the other chapter members looked to me.

When out shopping for groceries, furniture, or even a new car, I have discovered that the collar can produce one of four effects. First, there are those who scowl at me and who are unwaveringly certain that I will sexually molest any male child, twelve-years-old or younger without hesitation. I have had more than one mother who, walking toward me, hand-in-hand with their child, instinctively moved their child to the other side, so as to place themselves between me and the child. *- I always want to shout, "I'm Episcopalian!" but mostly I look elsewhere for fear of the recriminating stares.* The second type are those who have fear - *always the fear* - that I have X-ray vision, which provides me with the supernatural gift of looking within their souls and discerning their deepest sins. These stare, but quickly avert their eyes for fear of being called out and condemned to the fires of hell for all eternity. Third, you have the ones who - *and who typically are adorned in baby blue suits* - just stare, clearly having been raised in some lower form of protestantism to which a priest in a collar is akin to Telly Savalas with hair. Finally, there are the, "Oh, Father, how can I help you," and

"Oh, Father, it's so nice to have you with us," and "Oh, Father...."

Tonight, following the opening prayer, I added a new effect that the collar produces: "Save us!" I was not prepared for this mentally or emotionally, not to mention, I had only been a priest for fourteen months. I'm the curate, remember? The biggest decision they allow me to make is whether we take the youth group for burgers or pizza *and even then I'm generally out voted.*

"Mike, I've put together an agenda," I begin, with some apprehension, "but it's just the basics. In the absence of the Dean... I guess the chapter president is the one that should take the lead from here."

"What? No," Mike said, looking around at the other members for support. "This one is out of my league. You're the one with the training for this sort of thing."

They all nodded in agreement and turned back to me.

For the record, I managed to sneak through Hebrew and Greek (church history was a bear as well), but I succeeded pretty well in the other courses in seminary, and I can assure you with one hundred percent certainty, there was never a single course titled, "The Bishop is Dead, the Dean is Murdered, and the Secretary and Custodian have been Brutally Attacked."

Not only was I not prepared to lead in this situation, but I was also more than a little surprised that Mike had ceded control so rapidly. Under normal circumstances, he was often difficult to reign in.

It is then, looking from one to the next that I notice that Hank Slidell and Janine Kline are not present.

"Has anyone seen Hank? Janine?"

They all look to one another, but no answer.

"Well...." Liturgy. Routine. These meetings had a very specific flow. "The first order of business is to approve the minutes of our last meeting."

There were no words spoken, but the sudden rustling of papers was a sure indication of agreement. The minutes. Yes. The minutes. That is where our meetings begin. None of those gathered had any inkling of what to do, but reading and approving the minutes gave us all a specific task that could be accomplished. It was reassuring. That was followed by the Treasurer's report and even though Hank was not present, it took our minds off the twenty foot elephant that was standing on the highly polished mahogany conference table. From there, we discussed the need to keep the press cordoned off to certain areas. *They had been trampling the flowers as much as they had trampled the reputations of so many politicians and other unfortunates who had been living their fifteen minutes.* Following this was an enthusiastic discussion on providing Miss Avery and Jimmy with meals during their recuperations, which led to a sincere conversation on upgrading the security for the church.

"With all those people out there - *clearly indicating the invading hordes of 'Them!'*" - one of the more junior members of chapter said, "we've got to protect the women and children."

Oh, my...

Before someone suggested we dig a mote and build a wall, I moved the conversation along to the elephant. I wasn't so sure that I was ready, but they seemed to be. An organized discussion and Robert's Rules of Order had somehow managed to accomplish what an opening prayer had not. *Then again, perhaps the prayer...*

"I have been keeping in continuous contact with the police through Detective Thomas Stavlo," I began. "Here is what we know so far."

From there I filled in all the details and squashed as many rumors as I could, but did not go into the discussion of the $200,000 or a certain resident of the Hedge. Concerning the murder and other events, there was speculation, but by the time the meeting was drawing to a close, we all agreed that the crimes made no sense. Eventually, silence fell as they allowed the details to settle. It wasn't much of a meeting and little was actually accomplished, but we experienced that spiritual act of fellowship. If only for a moment, we knew that we were not alone in the dark.

When all looked up, after searching their own souls, I began, "Our Father...."

It was once explained to me that if we were to actually pray that prayer as it was intended, it would take us all day. That evening, I understood how that could be.

Following the meeting, the members were hesitant to leave, the fellowship and sense of having something to do in the midst of the chaos was cathartic. Eventually, they left together, all but a few agreeing to meet for a glass of wine at a local pub. Mike held back, but said he would join them. He followed me as I went through my nightly routine of checking lights, wiggling toilet handles, and locking doors.

"Just to be on the safe side. If we have one more act of violence around here, we may have to call the bishop... well he's dead... but somebody for an exorcist." He laughed, but he didn't seem to think it was actually all that funny. Completing the circuit, we ended in the office.

"Father, that was a good meeting."

I nodded in agreement.

"I don't know that we accomplished much, but we got together and moved forward, but I was wondering," he said, looking past me to the office door and hallway, insuring that we were still alone, "have you heard from Hank or Janine? It's not like either one to miss."

"No. I was kinda hoping you had."

"She's his office manager...."

"Oh? I didn't know that."

"Yeah. Has been for several years now. I didn't mention it during the meeting because I didn't want to worry anyone, but when I called today to check on some matters for our place, we use their services, the gal who answered the phone said that neither one came in today and they hadn't heard from either. She didn't seem too worried, but thought it odd. Anyhow, I just thought maybe you had heard from them."

I could just see Stavlo putting out an A.P.B. - *my days of watching Dragnet, Adam-12, and COPS were paying off* - as soon as he heard.

"No, but I am a bit surprised," I said, hoping my expression didn't show exactly how surprised I was.

"Alright," he said, disappointed, then added, "Say, I'm headed down to have a drink with the chapter. Need a lift? I'll have you home within an hour. Cassy's going to be looking for me soon."

"You know, I think I'm going to pass. The Zekester is waiting on me and honestly, I'm beat."

"I hear ya. Alright," he said, turning to go, "if you change your mind, you know where to find us."

"Thanks."

"G'night," he said, waving as he left the office, but then turned. "If you do hear from Hank or Janine, would you let me know? Just want to make sure they're OK."

"Will do. You do the same."

"Roger that," and he was off.

I thought about grabbing a few things out of my closet, but quickly changed my mind. I slapped the last two light switches on the way out and started crossing the lawn to the rectory. That's when I saw them. That proverbial large hand gripped my chest as I tried to comprehend.

"You gotta be kiddin' me," I said to the night and the brake lights.

MONDAY 9:37 P.M.

"That make and model has got to be one of the most popular automobiles in the country. It could have been anyone," I said to Stavlo, who hadn't sat down since he arrived. And for the tenth time I said, "And Mike Leigh didn't kill Dean Harris." My soul so desperately needed to believe this. "There is absolutely no motive!"

"Padre, I think we would all be amazed at what goes on in the darker corners of each other's minds. Motives are often far less creative than we would like to think."

"Yeah, yeah. Boy with tennis shoes, but we're talking about Mike Leigh here. He is very well respected in the church and the community."

"Tell me again what you remember."

"What?" *Lord, him with his subject transitions were impossible.* "Well, we had just finished chapter...."

"No. Not tonight. The night of the murder."

"Oh. Well... not much."

"Try."

"I heard a noise...."

"The under-passage door banging?"

"Right. I heard the door bang and realized I wasn't alone. I don't know why, but I took off after whoever it was. I heard them go out the staff parking lot door...."

"You didn't mention that before."

"What?"

"That you heard them exit the staff exit."

"Oh. Really?"

He only stared.

"Right. So I heard them exit that door ahead of me and thought I could catch up to them if I went out the east cloister door by the offices, but even as I was about to hit the crash bar, I remembered that it was locked. Fumble for my keys and by the time I fish them out, get the door unlocked and outside, whoever it was is already driving helter-skelter out of the parking lot. All I saw were the brake lights as they headed out the exit."

"Which way did they go?"

"Um... right."

"Which way did Leigh go tonight?"

"Left, but...," I trailed off.

"But what?"

"He was headed to the pub," I didn't want to say it and only did after hesitating, "but he would likely go right, otherwise. He lives that way, but he didn't do it," I add, almost shouting.

Silence enters the room. I sit absently rubbing on Z-Boy as Stavlo stares out the window towards the church. There are now three fronts to the investigation, Elvis, Hank, and Mike. Even though I had earlier somewhat convicted Hank in my heart, I can't bring myself to believe either of the church members is guilty, but the thought of Mike reminds me of that other detail.

"Oh."

"There's a clue waiting to be shared," he said, without turning.

There are all sorts of clergy wellness hocus pocus voodoo goings on in the ecclesiastical world that I avoid like I avoid rose vestments on Guadette Sunday, but the man should be aware that this is a bit more stressful than listening to Granma Angeline's confession on Saturday evening.

"I'm doing my best here," I say to his back.

"I know, Padre," he said turning, "but this entire business makes me a bit cranky. Sorry," he says, finally taking a seat on the couch, "What have you got?"

"Have you met Janine Kline?"

"Names familiar, but I don't think so."

"She is a member of the chapter. Last one to leave the Sunday service following Dean Harris' funeral."

"Right. Pretty girl."

"Yes. Well, she is the office manager down at Hank's firm. Has been for years."

"Ok," he said, sitting up to the edge of his seat.

"Neither one of them were at chapter tonight and, according to Mike, neither one of them were at work today."

"How did he know?"

"Called on some business with Hank. Secretary that answered said they were both out. No idea where they were."

"Well, they could be in Bolivia by now," he said, standing and pulling out his cell phone.

Based on the call, I had been spot on with the A.P.B. *Reverend Detective, let's not get carried away.*

No sooner had he hung up and my phone was ringing. For a priest, any call after 10:00 p.m. is never really good. I listen, take a few quick notes, then end the call. I've forgotten he was even in the room, so when Stavlo speaks, I jump.

"Problem?"

"Thirty-nine year old mom of three. Breast cancer. Not expected to make it through the night. Yes. Problem," I say flatly and stand. "I've got to go."

"I'll drive you," he said, fishing the keys out of his pocket.

"That's really not necessary, I could be there awhile."

"Padre, I don't mean to worry you, but almost every member of the staff of St. Matthew's has been attacked. I don't need another of you in that category."

"I'm fine," I say, my confidence shot before the words exit my mouth.

"So was the Dean, Miss Avery, and Jimmy."

I wanted to say, 'You're just being paranoid,' but he was right and now I was starting to feel a bit so.

We drive in silence, both of us focused on our work.

Reese Payne was one of those delightful ladies who never

lost her smile. Her children were happy and her husband was happier. It was the family that everyone else only imagines exists, and only witnessed in the movies or some sitcom. Twelve months ago, Dean Harris allowed me the pleasure of baptizing Hannah, the youngest of Reese and Daniel's three daughters. It was my first baptism, and I didn't drop the baby, which had been my fear the entire week preceding and what had kept me awake most of the nights before.

We had practiced on baby dolls in seminary, but the baby doll never wiggled. Our professor's biggest warning: "Don't let that child get their feet on you! They'll launch like Sputnik. If Mama doesn't catch them, you're looking at a career ending event."

Seven months ago Reese had discovered a lump. She put off going to the doctor for a few more months, but it probably wouldn't have made any difference if she had gone sooner. There they all were, a beautiful young family, and there it was, silently reaching in and killing her. They were stunned along with the entire congregation. We all went into denial, but soon afterwards it began taking its toll on her. First there were the dark circles under her eyes, but when I had visited her last week, she was emaciated, those beautiful gray eyes of hers deeply sunken in. When I came in the door that day a week ago, Daniel looked up at me in such a way that I knew he fully expected me to perform a miracle, but there were no miracles coming, only words of comfort and peace.

As the doors to the hospital slid quietly open, I entered my pastoral mode. It may seem detached to some, but it is a place I enter in order to do what I have been called to. It's not easy or comforting to others to give last rites, while bawling with everyone else. The priest, at times like this, is called to be the calming presence. He or she can grieve later, with a glass of wine, and a poodle to pet.

We encountered Nancy as she was leaving, but she must have heard the news already.

"She's such a dear, Father."

"Yes. Yes she is. We will do what we can," I say, taking

both her hands in mine, "we will pray."

"Yes, Father," she said, and gave me a quick hug. The scowl returned when she saw Stavlo, but she said nothing.

The receptionist directed us to room 675. It was never advertised as such, but that is where they moved you to die in as much peace as the hospital could garner.

"I'll be right out here," he said, as we approached the door.

"Thanks, but it may be awhile."

"I've got time, Father."

The lights were down when I entered the room. Daniel was the only one there. He sat beside his wife, holding her hand and speaking to her softly. She gave no sign of hearing. He looked up as I came within the small glow of the bedside light.

"Father." His voice was flat. He was angry with God and as God's representative, he was angry with me. "This isn't how it was supposed to be. We went to church. We prayed. We're good people," he blurted. Angry tears streaming down his face.

"Yes, Daniel. And you still are. What is happening is not a judgment on you," I said, taking a seat across the bed and across Reese from him. "This just is."

I love most of what I do as a priest, but there are no words for times like this.

We spent the next three hours visiting. There were tears, stories, some laughs, and then silence, except for the hissing of oxygen and Reese's occasional raspy breath. Then, even that was silent.

Following a flurry of activity with nurses and doctors coming and going, the silence returned. Daniel nodded. We prayed.

"Depart, O Christian soul, out of this world...," I had to stop to keep my voice from breaking. Father Professional was struggling, but then it was Daniel's turn to comfort. He reached across his wife's body and placed a hand on my arm.

"We can do this."

"Yes, we can. 'Depart, O Christian soul....'"

Mike and I followed the funeral home attendants down the service elevator and watched with our arms around each other, as they loaded the gurney and Reese into the coach. We watched until they were out of site.

"Need a ride home?"

"No. I'll be OK. I do need to get home to the girls, though. My mom has been watching them, but Father," he said, looking over my shoulder, "I'm just curious. Whose the pit bull that's been following you around?"

I had forgotten that Stavlo was there.

"Him. He's a friend."

"Good to have friends," he said, and with a quick hug, he made his way toward his car.

I looked at my watch - 3:17 a.m.

"I don't know what you get paid," Stavlo said, coming up peacefully beside me, "but it ain't enough."

"Honestly," I answer, accepting the cup of coffee he offered, "I'd do it for free.

'For a day in your courts is better
   than a thousand elsewhere.
I would rather be a doorkeeper in the house of
   my God than live in the tents of wickedness.'"

"Who said that?"

"Some guy named David."

"I might like to read some of his stuff," he commented, as we made our way back to his car.

"I have a copy of his book. I'll loan it to you."

"Thanks, Padre."

I wasn't certain if King David, or whoever had written Psalm 84, would appreciate the inspired word of God being referred to as 'stuff,' but it was too late to argue.

Zekey was happy to see me when I got home, but was asleep and quietly snoring before I had even brushed my teeth. The week just got busier with Reese's funeral, but that was OK. It is one of the many reasons the church is here. To speak life, even in death.

DAMN IT!

"Damn it! Answer your phone," he said, jabbing the end button on his.

It had been so long since he had last fallen in love that the emotions he was currently experiencing reminded him of being a teenager. God, how good it was to be alive again, even if it hurt.

Maybe they had been wrong. There may still be a way to make it work.

"What are you doing down here?"

"Shi... you scared the mess out of me!"

"What are you doing?" she repeated, with impatient bitterness.

"Just.. just chillin'."

"Chillin'!" she said with that smile that was only hatred. "What are you? Twelve?"

Sixteen.

"Just be sure to lock the doors when you decide to come up and don't leave that glass in the sink for me to have to put away tomorrow."

He kept from verbally cursing her, oh, but so many angry words rushed through his mind.

"God...," he whispered to himself, after she had stomped back up the stairs, but he did not believe any help would be coming from that direction.

When he thought it was safe, he tried the number again.

No answer.

"Damn it."

TUESDAY - 6:42 A.M.

I chased him through the west cloister, but remembering the east cloister exit was locked, I continued on and turned left towards the offices. My heart took an extra beat as I saw him just going through the south exit into the staff parking lot. I was only a few steps behind and when he heard me crash through the door, he turned, and without stopping, he came directly at me, and raised the stone paver to strike a killing blow.

"Mike! Stop!" I shouted, raising my hands to ward off the blow.

I felt the blow on my chest instead. It was much softer than I had anticipated. It came again, but this time was accompanied by a warm and rather smelly breath in my face. I opened my eyes.

At this angle, Zekey Boy's nose is massive, yet I was thankful that he had woken me when he did. His cold nose on my cheek was much more preferable than getting smacked by Mike.

"He didn't do it," I said to Z, which only got him to take off for the door. Seeing the clock, I was surprised he had let me sleep this long.

"Everybody's got their routines," I say, letting him out after first making sure there was nothing of interest to chase down still lingering in the lawn. He bolted out and headed to the men's. He was back before the last kibble was in his bowl.

The morning prayer and coffee did nothing to remove the sand from my eyes, but I refused to complain. A bit of weariness is nothing compared to waking up and having to explain to three young daughters why mommy won't be coming home again.

"8:02 Zekey. It doesn't matter that we were up late, time for work. Have a nice nap, ya' bum." No sooner had I locked the door, than my phone rang. Quickly turning and unlocking the door I ran back in, only to find the dog standing on the coffee table and looking out the widow.

"What the...."

He slinked down as though I hadn't seen him.

"We're going to have a discussion about that," I say, while picking up the reciever. "Hello. Father Anthony."

"Figured you'd still be sleeping."

"But you called anyways. How considerate."

"Look, Padre, I'm going to need to stop by and ask a few questions about our discussion last night. There are certain folks who need to provide some answers."

"He didn't do it."

"So you say. How about nine-ish?"

"How about ten-ish."

"Compromise?"

"See you then," I say, ending the call. Then looking at Zekey who is now in his chair, "Stay off the coffee table."

"That's tellin' him," I say, locking the door again and heading across the lawn to the church.

My initial thought upon entering the building, 'I should have brought Z.' At least he would have greeted anyone who was here, as it turned out, no one was, but it still didn't take long for me to get a case of the willies.

I tried to further prepare for the week, but it wasn't going to happen. I wandered the building and eventually found my way to the Courtyard.

I sat, I prayed.

Confession: I sat, I fell asleep.

Some noise brought me part way to the surface. A strong grip on my shoulder and a rather booming voice, sent me several feet above.

"You trying to be a victim here? You should at least lock

the door."

I'm uncertain as to whether or not I had just taken a swing at a police officer, but I did have to turn to Our Lady and beg forgiveness for the words that had crossed my lips in her presence.

"Ok, Chuckles," I say, turning back to Stavlo - *apparently a priest swearing rather fluently is humorous to some*. "Next time, you might want to consider announcing yourself."

"Sorry, Padre. I'm fairly certain you couldn't hear me over your own snores." He shoved a large cup of coffee at me. "You fall asleep in interesting places. Narcolepsy?"

I ignored him, but thanked him for the nectar.

"Do you live off this stuff?" I asked, giving him a cheers as well.

"Yes I do. I like it hot and black like my heart."

"You know," I say, as we walk back toward the offices, "you've got yourself convinced that you are such a hard case, but I'm not buying it. You would make a good priest."

"Padre, it is pretty early in the day to be smokin' crack."

"I'm serious. So many priest that I know have never experienced life. They prance around in their pretty robes like the Pharisees in the time of Jesus and not only think everyone should be as holy as them, but should also pay them great homage. In truth, they stifle the peoples faith and are generally more legalistic than a traffic court judge with hemorrhoids." *I'm fairly certain Mr. Stavlo snorted coffee through his nose.* "I prefer my priest to have lived a bit of life before they go telling me how to live mine. You," I say, stopping to fish out the keys to my closet, "would do a fine job."

"Father, you've got more faith than most of the people I know combined."

"You'd be surprised. There are a lot of days when I would prefer to sneak out the back door and keep walking. The word 'fraud' comes to mind far to often."

"And he thinks I should be a priest," he says, looking and gesturing upwards. "Padre, let's go see if we can catch a killer, then will work on your self-esteem and my calling in life."

"He didn't do it," I say, under my breath.

"So you keep telling me and you may be right, but he's not being one hundred percent truthful. He may not have killed Dean Harris, but it appears as though he was here that evening, he left in a hurry, and he's not being honest, otherwise he would've already come out with the info."

As much as I wanted to, I could come up with no argument against that.

"I've got four individuals I need to interview," he continued, settling into the one extra chair in my office, "Hank Slidell, Simon Presley, Janine Kline, and Mike Leigh. The whereabouts of Hank, Elvis, and Janine are currently unknown, so I've got to start with Mike. I know," he said, holding up his hands, "he didn't do it, so help me prove it. Give me some background on him before I have to find a quiet place to interview him, or haul him in and do the same."

With that, we hunkered down. I shared with him everything I knew about Mike Leigh and his family, which was the picture of a perfect father, husband, warden, and friend.

Stavlo listened without interruption. When I concluded, he leaned back in his chair, then forward again after a few minutes.

"That's the picture I expected you to paint. Probably mostly true, but there are shadows in everyone's life. You know that?"

"Yes."

"Padre, Mike's got a few shadows." He paused, mulling something over, then, "I'm going to share a few details that I probably shouldn't, but seeing as you're the one in the collar, I'm going to trust you."

"Unwise."

"I'll let you prove me wrong."

"Your call."

"On the night that Dean Harris was murdered, Mike Leigh stated that he was at a conference in Chicago."

"Right. He didn't get back until Saturday evening."

"True," he said, leaning forward, "but he didn't spend the night in Chicago. In fact, he didn't arrive at the conference until almost noon on Saturday. And it wasn't a conference. It was just a bunch of guys getting together at a sports bar to watch the games and drink beer."

"How do you know all this?"

"Because I'm very good at my job."

I did not doubt this for an instant. The image of Mike Leigh as father, husband, warden, friend tarnished a few shades.

Bishop Argus Preston was our Ascetical Theology professor in seminary. In addition to having a thing for Brigit Bardot, he was also very wise after having spent over sixty years as a cleric. In one of those moments when he was speaking to us as equals, he shared an insightful observation

"If you stay in a parish long enough, you will be able to look out over the congregation on a Sunday morning and know all the trials and sins that fill the sanctuary. This one has cancer and that one struggles with gambling. He drinks too much and hits his wife and children when he does, immediately regretting it. That one has a prison record that no one knows about and so on." Bishop Preston went on to explain that we could allow the burdens of others to rest upon us, but in doing so, we should expect to be overwhelmed. The alternative was to release them to God's care. Following Reese's death and now these revelations about Mike, I quickly recognized that I must learn how to practice what Bishop Preston had taught. A person could choke on so much intimate information and never taste clean air again.

We concluded our conversation long after the coffee had gone cold. I walked out to the parking lot with him and watching him drive off, looked to heaven and offered a silent prayer.

Holy Michael, the Archangel, defend us in battle. Be our safeguard against the wickedness and snares of the devil. May God rebuke him...

TUESDAY - 3:24 P.M

The phone call from the funeral home finally came. They would be meeting with Daniel tomorrow morning at 10:00 a.m. to plan the funeral for Reese. This I could handle - *I pray* - but I still had not heard from Stavlo.

Cassandra had been in most of the day to help in the office, answering the phone, preparing Sunday bulletins, and all the other necessary jobs to keep a church moving forward, but more than ninety percent of her time had been spent in my closet speculating on who might be behind all the violence. It is at times like this that I would prefer not to be a priest. I only want to yell at folks and tell them in very specific terms to go away - *I caught myself on more than one occasion on the brink of doing just that with Cassandra.* I am much more suited for a secular position where "The Man" in charge can be an ass and still draw a paycheck. *Then again, I'm always surprised at the number of clergy who can be the ass and still remain employed by the church.* My most recent urge to shout was resolved with the phone ringing. Cassandra darted out to answer, but hollered back after less than a minute - *one day she may learn to use the intercom.*

"Father, it's that policeman!"

"Finally," I say to myself, picking up the receiver. "Took you long enough."

"Any chance you could meet me down at the station?"

"You arrested him?"

"No, but I needed a statement and this is the one place where we can talk and not be overheard."

"Why do you need me? This sounds like your department." *Of course I'll go!* My heart is pounding and the junior detective is anxious for the details, but this is Mike and he is making an official statement.

"This one," Stavlo says in a quieter voice, "actually falls in both our departments."

"I'm on my way."

He hung up without a word. This wasn't going to be good.

She must have heard me hang up, because Cassandra was at the door as soon as I stood to leave.

"Oh...."

"Father, are you OK," she asked, taking a step closer - *which put her well within my personal space.*

Hunky-dory, Cassandra! Just on my way down to the police station to hear an official statement from your husband regarding the death of the Dean. Don't you worry though, he didn't do it.

"Oh...."

"Father?"

"Something has come up. Gotta go."

"Should I call Mike? He should have his cell with him."

"No," I say, perhaps a bit to loudly. "Something... unrelated."

She has more questions written across her face, but I sidestep around her before she can ask them.

"Father...."

"Please lock up after I leave. Thanks. Gotta run!"

This situation was like the cancer that killed Reese. Silently working its way into our body.

Twenty minutes later, the officer at the front desk was buzzing me through. Stavlo met me as I was walking through the door.

"What is this?" I ask, shaking hands and following in the direction he pointed.

"He asked to speak to you first before I say anything."

"Why?" I couldn't understand any of what was happening, but before he had time to answer, he opened the door to the stereotypical police interview room. Mike was sitting across a small table from us as we entered. Smoking had not been allowed in these places for years, but the smell and nicotine stains on the walls remained. When Mike looked up and saw me coming in behind Stavlo, he put his head in his hands and began to loudly sob. I looked to Stavlo for some explanation, but he only gestured to one of the two metal chairs on our side of the table.

"Mike?" I said, sitting down and reaching out to him. "What is this, Mike?"

"Oh, God," he said, looking up and catching my eye and then started with the sobbing again.

Stavlo disappeared for a minute, then returned with three cups of coffee, the smell of which told me was not near the quality he had become accustomed to or occasionally spoiled me with.

Setting a cup in front of us each, he said, "We'll work this out, Mike, but right now I need you to talk to the Reverend here and to me. The sooner it's out the sooner we can begin to work on what to do next. You're not in any more trouble than a half-pint lawyer won't be able to get you out of...."

My head snapped around to face Stavlo. He only held up a hand up to keep me silent.

"We'll work this out, but the Dean has been murdered and two other individuals have been attacked. We've got to get this sorted before anything else happens."

Still looking down at the table and after wiping his face, Mike nodded. Looking up, he said, "I hope that half-pint lawyer can also help me with my divorce. I'm ruined after this."

For one taste of clean air...

"Cassandra and I celebrated our tenth anniversary a little over a year ago. It was a good day, at least in the beginning," Mike said, looking up from his hands for a moment. "The new Chapter members had recently been elected at the annual church meeting, so we invited them along with their spouses, Dean Harris, and several other friends."

"Mike," Stavlo said, "we need to..."

Mike cut him off by holding up his hand.

"I know you want to hear what happened and this is where it began."

If he was going to make a confession, he was going to make a complete confession. Stavlo had to be patient.

"Father, you've probably noticed by now that when Cassandra gets to talking she can sometimes forget where the 'Off' switch is."

I gave him an understanding smile.

"Well, what you may not have noticed yet is that when she has a glass or two of wine, listening to her talk is like drinking from a fire hydrant. It can be a bit overwhelming. On that day, she had more that a couple of glasses and the topic of that rapid fire talking turned to me. It was harmless at first, but it wasn't long before everyone within earshot was wondering why she stayed married to me."

The anger was still evident.

"Me, I just smiled and laughed while the entire gathering became increasingly more uncomfortable. I suppose it was the typical 'guy' issues she was going on about at first: didn't help around the house, not a good listener, out with the boys too much, etc. All the fellas were having a few good guffaws at my expense, knowing all along that if their wives got going, the shoe would be on the other foot. The ladies, they also were good natured about it at first, throwing in a few 'Preach it, sister's' to keep her going."

No matter the jab, they always sting, yet knowing this does not stop us from returning the favor. How many relationships have been ruined, one pen prick at a time?

"Her routine was getting a bit tiring for everyone, but then it just got mean. By the time she got around to my performance in bed, folks were making excuses for having to leave early. Dean Harris was the last to leave. Cassandra had wandered off somewhere, I found her later sprawled out on the bed with her shoes still on, so Dean Harris made as if to help me with the clean up. He was a priest, but he always served like a deacon." *Remember that. Remember that.* "I was ready to be alone though, so I went, got his coat, and politely sent him on home. It was a Saturday night anyhow, and I know how early he got up on Sundays.

"I took my time cleaning, but I was fuming too." Raising his voice, "In my own house I had been made, by my wife, to feel like a festering sore on the backside of a mongrel dog. If this had been the first time, I probably could have let it go, but for several years now, this has been the norm. She normally kept it between us and it occasionally spilled out in front of the girls, but never had she been so nasty in front of others. Anyhow... I didn't sleep much that night. After cleaning the last of the party, I sat in my chair, all of Casandra's words repeating in my head. Then I remembered something. Something kind that one person had said.

"In the middle of everyone packing off that night there was only one who acknowledged the scene. She made ready to leave only a short time before Dean Harris, but couldn't find her coat, so I walked her to the front bedroom where we had tossed them all on the bed and then walked her to the front door. I was looking down as I opened the door, too damn embarrassed to want to look anyone in the eye, but then I feel this soft hand on my cheek. I look up and gaze into the eyes of one of the kindest people I've ever met. She stared me straight in the eye and said, 'You're a good man. Don't let her soil you.' Then, before turning to go, she kissed me lightly on the cheek. Nothing sexual, just caring and reassuring. Later that night, thinking of her words and that kiss, all the anger drained out of me, and I could think of nothing else... or anyone else.

"Over the course of the next several weeks, her words and that simple touch... It wasn't an obsession," he said, reaching for the right word, "it was a passion. A sense of finally finding what you've been looking for all your life.

"I know, Father," he said, surfacing from his memories, "it was sinful. Sinful thoughts. Just fantasies that I entertained and then acted on."

The pastoral side of me wanted to speak, but at this point, I was too overcome to think through it clearly, not to mention the lack of experience I had in this department, so I followed Stavlo's lead and remained silent.

"Even in my anger, I love my wife and my daughters. Cassandra and I have had a wonderful marriage, it was just one of those seasons when things weren't so good. We'd see our way through it, but in the middle of it... In the middle of it, I set out to discover more about the lady behind the kind words and the soft kiss. I wasn't disappointed. I fell in love. She did too. It ended the night Dean Harris was killed, but I didn't know about his death until the following evening, just a few minutes before I called you."

"Who is she, Mike," I asked, finally finding my voice.

A sad smile.

"Janine. Janine Kline."

TUESDAY - 5:18 P.M.

The old joke tells of how nervous the new priest is about hearing confessions, so he asks his mentor to sit in on his sessions. The new priest hears a couple of confessions, then the mentor asks him to step out of the confessional for a few suggestions.

The mentor suggests, "Cross you arms over your chest, and rub your chin with one hand." The new priest complies.

"Now, while doing that, try saying things like, 'I see, yes, go on', and 'I understand. How did you feel about that?'" The new priest says those things.

The mentor concludes, "Now, don't you think that's a little better than slapping your knee and shouting, 'Hot damn! What happened next?'" Which was probably preferable to what comes out of my mouth.

"Holy sh…"

"Language, Padre."

"I'm so sorry, Mike," I said, my face heating up with embarrassment. "Not one of my better pastoral moments."

"It's OK. I've been saying it for the last year, every time I consider what I've gotten myself into."

"Alright," Stavlo says, "before you go on, do you know where Janine is? She's been missing for several days now."

"No," he said, a look of concern crossing his face. "I've tried to call her a dozen times, but she never answered. I figured she just didn't want to talk to me. Missing?"

"Yeah," I say. "She and…"

"Let's continue," Stavlo says, interrupting me before I could mention Hank Slidell.

Junior detective made an error. It wouldn't be his last.

Mike looks from one to the other of us.

"Is she OK?"

"There is nothing to indicate otherwise," Stavlo says then, "Please continue."

He was reluctant without knowing more about what was going on with Janine, but picked up his story.

"I'm sorry to say, Father, but it really all started with us visiting during coffee hour after Sunday services. I suppose that'll get me an extra hot fire in the end?"

"I know someone who can definitely get you out that one," I tell him without hesitation.

"I'm not so sure about that anymore."

"I am."

He continues.

"From there we graduated to the occasional lunch, but even from the first real conversation we had, I think we both knew where it was headed, and we both wanted it to stop, but there was a part of us that wanted to be together more. It wasn't long before I had an increasing number of late night meetings and overnight conferences. If Cassandra suspected something, she didn't let on or she just didn't care. I was out from under foot. I think somewhere in my soul I knew better, but by then, I didn't want to hear it. I wanted to be with Janine. It's that complicated or that simple, however you want to look at it."

"So," Stavlo said, pulling out his pad and pen, "on the night Dean Harris was murdered you were attending an overnight 'conference' with Janine?"

"Yes." He hung his head again.

"Where?"

Mike gave him the name of a hotel outside of the city.

"Will I be able to verify this?"

"Yes. I always paid, but we used Janine's credit card so that it wouldn't show up on my home account."

"Go on."

"We both knew that it had to end." Turning to me he said, "As pathetic as it sounds, we both knew we were sinning, Father.

We both knew what we were doing was wrong. It finally got to me enough that I made an appointment with Dean Harris a few weeks before he died. I came in to resign as Chapter President. I didn't believe I was fit to hold such a position in the church given... all this," he said with a wave of the hand. "Dean Harris was pretty amazing when it came to matters of the soul, so - and this was not my intention when I went in - but I ended up confessing everything to him. I mean, a proper confession like you see in the movies. Did you know we have that in the prayer book, Father?"

"They did mention it in seminary."

"Well, it was a first for me, but Dean Harris saw a lot more than he let on. Without me even saying anything about Janine, he knew it was what I needed. He was right and it gave me the resolve I needed to help Janine and I get out of the pit we had dug for ourselves.

"The next two weeks really were busy at work. I didn't even see much of Cassandra and the girls, so what little contact I had with Janine was just a few messages. We made plans to meet the Friday night of the Dean's murder. God, what a mess. We made plans and I let on that it needed to be our last."

"How did she respond to that," Stavlo asked.

"Sad. Who am I kidding? We were both sad, but like I said, we both knew it wasn't right. We planned for a fun evening and a goodbye. That didn't work out either. Janine was running late, which gave me about two drinks too many in the bar while I waited. Instead of going out for dinner, we went up to the room and talked. We talked, we cried, we laughed, but when I told her that I had made a confession to Dean Harris, she became very unsettled. I suppose I shouldn't have mentioned any names, but in the process of my confession I said Janine's name - He knew by the way. Can you believe that? He said it was rather obvious given the way we started acting toward one another, especially at Chapter meetings."

I could have learned so much from him.

"Anyhow, when I told Janine that bit, she got angry. She

had every right to. It wasn't my place to confess for her. She settled after a bit, but she never stopped thinking after that. You could see her mind racing. So while her mind raced, I had another drink."

"Was Janine drinking?" Stavlo asked.

"Um... No. I fell asleep in the chair at some point and didn't wake up until morning. Too much scotch. Janine was gone, can't say that I blame her, but I noticed that she had poured herself a glass of wine from the bottle I brought for her. She may have had a sip, but that's all."

Mike's second confession seemed to have ended. After a minute of silence, Stavlo stood and headed for the door.

"I'll be back."

Now he's Schwarzenegger.

"Coffee," I said, before he pulled the door closed.

"Yep."

"Where's Janine?" Mike asked in a hushed voice.

"I was really hoping you could tell us."

He shook his head.

I made several false starts in my head on something to say, but all my fourteen months of wisdom as a priest told me to keep it shut. For a change, I listened.

"Zekey," I said suddenly, looking up at the old steel mesh enclosed clock on the wall.

"What's wrong?"

"Nothing that some 409 and a mop won't fix," I say, and return to the silence.

Stavlo returned with more coffee.

"Ok, Mike, you say you fell asleep in the chair, but you see, that's where I have a little bit of a problem. Statistically speaking, you wouldn't be the first person to commit a murder while in an alcoholic blackout. In fact," he said, leaning forward for emphasis, "almost 40% of the homicides in this country had alcohol consumption as a contributing factor. Is it possible that you had a change of heart..."

Mike had already started shaking his head before Stavlo

had completed the sentence.

"...regarding your confession to Dean Harris and decided it was best to erase it?"

"No!" he shouted, jumping up and backwards, toppling his chair. "I would never!"

Stavlo stood very slowly. I got the impression he had practiced this move on more than one occasion, and the desired effect was immediate. Like a chastised schoolboy, Mike righted his chair and took his seat without a word. Stavlo followed.

Turning to me, Mike said, "Father, please tell him. Tell him I'm not the type of person to do something like that. Please," he added, turning back to the Lieutenant.

"Mike, I've told him over and over that you didn't do it. I'm sticking with that, but you have to see how this looks. Help him understand."

"I can't. I don't understand, myself. Father," he said, his eyes opening wide, "could I have done this? Could I have killed Dean Harris? Oh, God..."

A knock at the door.

After a moment, Stavlo stood and answered. Seeing who it was, he stepped out and closed the door.

"Mike," I said, reaching out and taking his hand. He only shook his head without looking up. "Mike, we're going to get through this. You are going to get through this. It won't be easy, but...."

Stavlo came back in, the tiredness in his face seeming to almost overcome him in the last few minutes.

"Mike," he said, in a more formal tone than before, "do you remember me asking for your permission to search your car when you came in?"

"Yes."

"Mike, would you state one more time that you agree to having your car searched?"

"Yes," more hesitantly. "It's OK... what's wrong?"

"Mike, there is evidence of blood on the drivers side front seat of your car. Looks like someone has tried to clean it up, but did so in a hurry. Mike, do you know if you or anyone else has ever been involved in accident and gotten in the front seat of your car while bleeding?"

"No," he said, looking anxiously back and forth between Stavlo and I.

"So you've no explanation as to how blood could have gotten in your car?"

"No."

"Mike, were you aware that Dean Harris carried with him a small black book that he used for jotting down notes and thoughts?"

Mike almost smiled.

"Yeah. Everybody knew about the Dean's little black book. We always use to guess about what he was writing. I don't know that anyone has every seen its content."

"Have you ever handled it yourself?"

"No. Never."

"Did you know that it has been missing since the night of the Dean's murder?"

"Yes. I think I heard that. The ladies were keeping an eye out for it as they cleaned the office after the break-in. Right?" He asked, looking over to me.

I nodded.

"What has this got...," but he trailed off as Stavlo pulled out an evidence bag containing a small black book. Streaks of blood clearly evident through the plastic bag on the edges of the pages. Stavlo placed it in the center of the table.

"Mike, can you explain to me how this came to be in your car?"

TUESDAY 6:17 P.M.

Mike and I stared at the small black book entombed in the evidence bag. Stavlo sat staring at Mike, waiting for some reply.

"I... where?"

"In your car down between the console and driver's seat." No emotion. Only the facts.

While we sat in silence, Stavlo pulled a pair of latex gloves out of his pocket and put them on. Carefully opening the bag and exhuming the book, he turned to me.

"Father, does this appear to be Dean Harris' book?"

"Yes. It looks like it."

Opening the book and showing me a few pages, he asked, "Do you recognize this as Dean Harris' handwriting?"

The Dean's handwriting was worse than mine and I recognized it immediately. I nodded.

"Mike, we'll confirm all this, but right now I'm 100% certain that this is the Dean's book and that the blood on it and in your car is the Dean's blood. I'm going to ask you again and I'd like for you to think about this real hard before you answer: do you have any idea how either the blood or this book ended up in your car?"

Without hesitation, "No," he said flatly, still staring in disbelief.

Stavlo returned the book to the evidence bag, sealed the bag, and removed the gloves, casually pitching them toward a nearby trash can. One missed and the other hung half in and half out of the can.

"Never was good at ball," he said, standing and picking

up the gloves, then depositing them both in the trash can with a dunking motion that seemed out of place, given the current circumstances.

"Mike, we're moving closer to the territory where you may want to be finding yourself that lawyer, but at this point, I don't recommend the half-pint variety. I'd be looking up a good and proper one."

"What?"

"Mike, I'm not arresting you at the moment, but I will be impounding your car. You are free to go. Don't go far," he said, as an afterthought.

"How am I supposed to get home?"

"Mr. Leigh, you figured out how to sneak around on your wife and kids for the last year, so I'm guessing you'll be able to figure out how to get a ride home."

"I'll give you a ride, Mike, unless you need me still?" I asked, turning to Stavlo.

"No."

That was it. Stavlo only stared straight ahead as we left the room. His treatment of Mike there at the end seemed overly harsh, but then, my mind had not yet completely crossed over from the loving father, Chapter President, devoted parishioner mode to the murder suspect mode; however, I do confess that it was on the precipice.

We walked silently out of the building.

"This way," I said, once we were outside, pointing in the direction of my car.

I had found a visitor space near the front door and just as we were about to climb in, I heard Stavlo calling from behind.

"Padre!" When he saw he had my attention and drawn near, "Change of plans. You need to come with me. We found her."

"Who?"

"Janine Kline."

"Where," Mike and I asked in unison.

"Tony's."

Mike and I looked at each other in confusion, then back to Stavlo.

"St. Anthony's Hospital. ICU. Unconscious. She's been a Jane Doe up until now. Brought in by ambulance three days ago."

"I've got to get to her," Mike said, "Father, can you...."

Stavlo cut him off.

"Mike, if I catch you anywhere near Miss Kline I will have you arrested on the spot. Do you understand?"

"I don't care! I have to see her. What happened to her?"

"Mike," I said, coming around to his side of the car, "go home. Wife. Daughters. Right now those are your three priorities. When I think it is appropriate, I will contact you and let you know how she's doing. Don't get yourself into anymore trouble here. Take my keys and go home. I'll get a ride home later."

"Take the Padre's advice, Mike. This is a line you do not want to cross. I'll get him home."

Mike took the keys I held out to him and, without a word, moved to the driver's side of the car.

"Mike," Stavlo said, pointing his finger at him just as he was getting into the car, "go straight home. Do not pass 'Go', do not collect $200."

Mike didn't answer, only got in the car and shut the door, which was not the response Stavlo was looking for. He moved quickly to Mike's window and tapped on the glass. Mike rolled down the window. I couldn't hear what was being said but didn't need to. The somewhat defiant look on Mike's face faded quickly and was replaced with fear and tears.

Stavlo stood, patted the roof of the car and turned to me.

"Come on, Padre. We're gonna figure this...."

It was a colorful tirade. When he had finished and we were driving towards Tony's, I finally had the nerve to say what I had been thinking, ever since he had pulled out that small black book in the interview room.

"I may be the most naive individual you've ever met or as

thick as Zekey Boy, but he didn't do it."

Without looking in my direction, he responded, "Do you honestly think I would have let him go if I thought he had?"

"Oh."

"Someone has got it in for you all at that church and I don't know why, but I do know it's not Mike. I'll tell you this, though."

"What's that?"

"Imma get 'em. And they're not gonna like it when I do."

I let that clear the air before speaking again.

"What happened to Janine?"

"I'll fill you in on the way, but let's stop by your place first."

"Why?

"Let your beast out. Unless his bladder is larger than mine, he's probably sitting there with his legs crossed."

I could hear him howling as soon as I got out of the car.

"Crazy animal."

When I inserted the key in the lock the howling stopped. I expected to be greeted with his normal happy self, instead he passed by me without a sniff and went directly to Stavlo.

"You sorry piece...."

"Language," he said, as Z then headed to the men's. "Although," he said grinning, "he does have a bit of an attitude."

"Just remember who feeds you," I said to the back of the ungrateful animal as he disappeared around the corner. I was about to turn and go in, but Stavlo, looking intently through the front door, grabbed me by the shoulders and moved me off the sidewalk.

"Stay here," he said, as he reached under that fishing vest of his and drew an intimidating piece of equipment of the 9mm variety.

"Hey, wait," I began, but ended by staring with my mouth open as I looked into the war zone of my living room. "What the hell, Zeke?" I said, shouting around the corner of the house. "It wasn't that long."

"It wasn't him," came Stavlo's voice from somewhere in-side. "Stay there and keep himself out."

"What do you mean, it wasn't… O, Lord, this has got to stop," now understanding what was happening.

"Yes, it does."

He was already on his phone as he was coming back out the door, pulling it closed behind him.

"They're after something," I said, as he passed.

"Yes, and they don't know we already have it."

"Have what? Have what?" I asked again when he didn't turn.

After a few moments it hit me.

"Seriously?" *He only wrote sermon notes and appointments in it.*

As Stavlo finished his phone call, Dumb Dumb came back around the corner of the house.

"Not much of a guard dog are you," I remarked as he once again passed me by without a glance and went to Stavlo for another scrub behind the ears. "Not very dang loyal either, ya mutt."

"You still want to go to the hospital or stay here? There's a team coming over to go over the house."

"I'll go with, but we need to do something with himself." *Did the dog just glare at me?*

"We'll drop him at my place. It's on the way."

"He'll get on the couch and drink out of the toilet."

"Trust me, he can't hurt the couch and that would go a long ways toward cleaning the toilet."

"Live alone, do ya?"

"For the last few years," he said, sounding a bit disap-pointed.

"Were you married?"

"We'll close the bathroom door and put some water down for him. He'll be fine and can't hurt a thing."

That wasn't even a smooth change of subject. And I may not be the wisest priest on the cloister, but I know when to drop a subject.

"Come on, Killer. Got a new coffee table for you to check out."

"There are also some uniformed officers on their way to Janine's residence," he said, as we pulled out onto the main road. I don't know what they'll find if anything. If they do, they'll call in the specialist."

"Why?"

"Janine was found early Thursday morning, around 3:00 a.m., on the wrong side of town. She was half naked, severely beaten..."

"O, God."

"Not the worst of it, she had also been stabbed."

"O, God." *These were not the statements of some automaton, these were the only prayers I could think to say.*

"The beatings and stab wound were bad, but could have been much worse. She will survive, but the investigative team determined that she had been ejected... pushed out of a moving vehicle. She was probably unconscious at the time, but that appears to have been when she got the hardest knock on her head. There has been excessive swelling, which has led to her deepened unconscious state.

"You taking all this in?" He asked, with a quick glance away from the road.

"No."

"Alright. As I said, she was half naked and on the wrong side of town when they found her. She had no I.D. It is unfortunate, but the truth, the investigators assumed she was a 'working girl' that had picked up the wrong guy and treated the case as such. That doesn't mean they didn't put everything into it, but it does mean they didn't plan on too many leads or breaks in the case."

"How'd they identify her then," I asked, as we pulled into the hospital parking lot.

"Pure dumb luck. Nurse who works four on and three off

happened to come on shift. Turns out, she's a member of your congregation."

"Rachel Costin?"

"That's the one. Even through the bruises and bandages, Rachel was able to identify Janine. Shocked, she looked at the chart. Two and two. The police were called."

"Is it always like that on *that* side of town?"

"Don't judge," he said as he pulled into a parking place.

"No."

We sat for a minute with the engine running.

"I read a book on the forest fires that take over the Rockies during the summer. These fires break out in Montana, Utah, Colorado. Burn hundreds of squares miles in the process. There's these guys, Smokejumpers, that drop into the middle of these fires and fight them with everything they've got. Occasionally though, they'll have what they call a blowout. Consumes the entire side of mountain in seconds. Soil melts. Trees don't burn. They incinerate or just explode. The Smokejumpers are in the middle of all that hell and they have these fire resistant blankets that they have less than seconds to get covered with before they're incinerated. Even if they do, they don't always make it." He shakes his head, even now, trying to comprehend such an event and such heroics.

"Padre," he says, as he kills the engine and opens the door, "we're under the blankets."

He got out before I had the opportunity to respond. Just as well, I didn't know what to say.

POISONED OAK

Cassandra was working in the front flower bed when Mike pulled up. She stood and smiled at seeing Father Anthony's car, but then frowned and went back to her weeding when she saw that it was only Mike.

He sat there for a minute or two, looking without seeing and trying to arrange it all in his head. It was all over. Maybe just drive into the garage, close the door and let the motor keep running. Maybe just drive away. Start over somewhere. He'd always thought how peaceful it would be to get out of the race, out of the family and be a night security guard in some anonymous town. Maybe find that relationship with God he had had once before. Maybe find some peace. Vows. The girls. The girls. They were never going to understand this. Responsibilities. Mortgage.

He was shocked out of his thoughts by Cassandra impatiently tapping on the driver's window with the handle of her weeding trowel. He must have been sitting there longer than he thought.

"You scared me," he said with a half smile, rolling down the window.

"Are you having a stroke?"

"No, just a think."

"Fine." She turned and returned to her flower beds.

He closed the window and killed the motor. As he approached, she spoke without looking up.

"Have a wreck?"

"No. A bit more interesting than that."

She went back to her weeding without asking. The silence darkened.

"Either say what you want to say or find somewhere else to be. It's irritating to have you just standing there."

"We use to enjoy being together. Just hanging out."

"Yeah," she said, ramming her spade into the ground and turning to face him, "we also use to be in love."

Enough.

"My car has been impounded by the police...."

"Did you get a DUI! You stupid...."

"I am being investigated for the murder of Dean Harris."

She was stunned into silence.

"They found blood on the driver's side of the car and the Dean's little black book, also covered in blood. They believe that it is the Dean's blood and and they are probably right. I've no idea how it got there."

Still nothing from her. Only a cool silence... and the hint of a smile?

"The night of the Dean's murder, when I had that meeting in Chicago, I wasn't really in Chicago...."

"You were with that little tart you've been running around with for... how long now?"

"A year."

"A year! Ha," she blurted out, "I thought it was only for nine months. Guess your chickens have come home to roost," she said with a broad nasty grin. Then turned and went back to her weeding.

"You knew?"

"You think you're so clever," she said sarcastically, while working on a particularly stubborn Dandelion. "Big shot business man, Chapter president hypocrite of the church, of course I knew."

"Have you been drinking?"

"Have I been drinking? Well, of course I have." She reached behind one of the shrubs, retrieved a half empty bottle of wine and took a swig. "And I'll tell you another thing: you see all this," gesturing toward the house and yard, "it will all be mine. You and your little friend aren't taking me down with you. Go. Go figure this one out on your own."

He started to leave, but turned back.

"If you knew, why didn't you ever say anything?"

That nasty smile again.

"I figured if you were satisfied in that department, then I wouldn't have to deal with it. I was right too, wasn't I?"

"You're always right, Cassandra. Never been wrong in your life."

The rest of the conversation made quite a show for the neighbors, but what Mike was mostly thankful for was that the girls were out. They didn't need to witness the growing cavern of disdain between their parents.

The conversation ended when Cassandra let sail the wine bottle, narrowly missing Mike's head, but covering his face in it's content as it whisked by. It came to rest at the base of an old oak tree that had been the centerpiece of their yard for all these years. Several years back they had to start trimming dead branches from it. Concerned that it might be dying they had called in a specialist who told them that it was in fact dying. Most likely poisoned from the runoff of the surrounding area.

TUESDAY 7:22 P.M.

Stavlo and I make our way to the ICU wing on the fifth floor of St. Anthony's. A small sign on the door instructed all visitors to call the nurses' desk before entering. I lifted the receiver of the white phone next to the door.

"ICU Nurses' Desk."

"This is Fr. Anthony Savel and Detective Thomas Stavlo. Could we come in and see Janine Kline?"

"I'm sorry, Fr. Anthony, you can come back for a few minutes, but we do not want to place too much stress on Miss Kline at this point. She only woke up this afternoon and is still a bit fuzzy. Room 518. Only a few minutes, Father."

"Certainly. Thank you."

"She's awake?" Stavlo asked before I had even hung up.

"Yes, but you can't come in. They've only given me a couple of minutes."

"I need to talk to her."

"Yes, again, but she needs to heal first. I'll find out when they think you can see her."

The doors hissed softly closed behind me. I had made more than a few visits to ICU and found Janine's room quickly. The lights were dim, but I could still see that she had her eyes open. When she saw me she gave me a soft smile.

"Father," she said, trying to push herself up in bed.

I stepped forward and placed my hand gently on her shoulder to settle her.

"Rest. I'm just here for a moment. Nurses orders."

"Father, this is my mother, Carolyn," she said, gesturing towards the shadowed corner of the room.

"I'm sorry, I didn't see you there," I said, reaching out to shake her hand.

"It's OK. They only let me stay if I agreed to let her rest as much as possible." But while her daughter was awake, she reached over and took Janine's hand in both of hers. "We've been so worried," tears trickling down her cheeks.

"I'm OK, mom. I'm OK."

"Yes." Turning to me, Carolyn said, "She's made remarkable progress. They're talking of a regular room by tomorrow."

"Wonderful news. Janine, they're going to kick me out pretty quickly. Could I say a prayer before I go?"

"Please, but...," she trailed off.

"But what?"

"I deserve this."

"Janine, hunny, don't say that," Carolyn said, leaning forward, gently touching her daughters face.

"No, I do."

"Janine," my turn to lean forward and look directly into her eyes, "I know why you think that."

Her mouth dropped open slightly and her eyes widened as she understood that I really did know. Carolyn looked back and forth between us, attempting to understand what was not being said. For now, I ignored her.

"I know why you think you deserve this, but you don't. That's not how it works and you know it. It's going to work out."

"But, Father...."

She was interrupted by the nurse who made it clear that I was overstaying my welcome. I assured her I would be leaving after a short prayer.

"One minute," she said, and held up her finger to emphasize the point in the event I didn't quite understand. "One."

We prayed for fifty seconds.

"It was nice to meet you, Carolyn." Turning to Janine again, "We'll talk soon. Rest."

"Bye, Father."

On my way out, I waved at the nurse and mouthed a 'thank you.' She nodded and went back to her own ministry.

"That was more than two minutes."

I pointed to my clerical collar.

"Well that's not right," Stavlo said, "I've got a badge that can't even get me through those doors."

"You should go shopping with me. Best service you'll ever get."

"That's not right."

"You already said that."

"Still true."

"Have you got a few more minutes? It's kind of late, but I would like to stop by and see Jimmy before we leave."

Miss Avery had been released the day before into the care of her sister whom she had nursed back to health all those years ago.

"No problem."

"Father A.," Jimmy said, as I entered the room. His smile at seeing me only faltered a little when he saw Stavlo come in behind me. "Officer," he said, nodding.

"Hey, Jimmy, you're looking a heck of a lot better," I said, and he was. All the medical equipment had been removed.

"Going home tomorrow morning," he said happily, leaning back in his bed and muting the TV that had been broadcasting the sports news. "Doc gave me a clean bill of health earlier this afternoon."

"That is excellent news," I say, joining in his joy.

"Doc says I may be able to get back to work as early as next Monday."

"Don't you worry about that. We'll manage, but I'll tell ya, it's taken a crew of ladies and some of the fellas to keep up with what you do. You're definitely missed."

"Thanks, Father. How's Miss Avery doing? She stopped in as she was leaving, but I haven't heard from her yet."

"She's doing just fine. Staying with her sister for the rest of the week, but planning to be back next Monday als...."

"What are you doing here?" someone asked angrily from the hall.

I didn't recognize the voice, but it was none too pleased. Stavlo gestured toward me as Nancy came into the room.

"Father," she said to me, much more civilly, glancing back at Stavlo, who watched without emotion. Those two had a strong dislike for one another. "Nice of you to call. He's out tomorrow. Dang fool thinks he's going back to work on Monday."

"Yes, wonderful news," I said, ignoring her second statement. "I was just telling him how much we've missed him around the church."

"Looking forward to it m'self 'cause I'm sick of this hospital room."

"Well, you're only going back when your well and it's safe." Another unpleasant glance at Stavlo.

"Any new developments on all this trouble?"

"Several, including Janine Kline."

"Janine?" asked Nancy, looking quickly at Jimmy then back to me.

"Um. Yeah. Sorry, I thought you had probably heard. She's upstairs in ICU. She was...."

"Involved in an accident," interjected Stavlo.

"Yeah, but," I said looking back at Stavlo to make sure junior detective wasn't about to step in it, "she's doing much better. Anyhow, there's plenty of time later to catch you up on all the news. For now, you just continue to rest and heal. This whole business has just been too much for all of us."

"You've got that right, Father."

We exchanged a few more pleasantries, Nancy and Stavlo both remaining quiet, but when Jimmy's attention kept being drawn back to the silent TV screen displaying the latest round of scores, I made ready to leave.

"Jimmy, I know you all attend a different church, but would you mind if I said a prayer with you before I go?"

"That would be real nice, Fa...."

"Our preacher already prayed over him," Nancy said, moving in as though to guard Jimmy so that I couldn't put some Episcopal whammy on him. Not my first time to experience this, but still off putting. I recovered quickly.

"Oh, that's great," I said, pulling back my hand. "Then I think we'll leave you to rest. You all let me know if there is anything that you need. The ladies at the church would be happy to fix some meals."

"We'll manage."

"Yeah," Jimmy said, frowning at his wife, "we'll be fine, but I'll let you know."

We said our goodbyes and headed out.

"I get the distinct impression that Nancy doesn't like you so much," I said, as Stavlo and I rode the elevator down.

"I get the distinct impression that Nancy doesn't like anyone."

As we walked to the car he stopped.

"What?"

"It's a bit late, but I could use a piece of pie. Interested?"

"M.O.O.N. That spells pie."

"Huh."

"Never mind. Pie sounds great, but I wouldn't mind a proper meal. From what I saw of my house, I'm going to be up awhile just trying to clear enough space for the boy and I to have a place to sleep."

"Right," he said, and retrieved his cellphone, placing a call on speed dial.

"Riley. Find anything?"

He listened.

"Keep me posted," he said, then ended the call. "Someone found their way in through a back window at your place. Made a mess. Same as the church offices. They're still looking for it, but we have it."

"True, but they don't know that. Do they?"

"I may need two pieces of pie."

The conversation at the diner had nothing to do with

murder, church, or crime. The time was spent in a heated debate over why key lime pie is a far superior pie to the cherry.
When I commented that the cherry filling that came out of a can
had a particularly unpleasant texture, I thought he was going to
draw his gun; however, we were in agreement that the coconut
meringue pie was a definite crowd pleaser and should be univer-
sally applauded.

"Looks like Mike returned your car," Stavlo said, as we
pulled into the rectory driveway after stopping by his place to
retrieve Z, who had been the perfect poodle houseguest.

"That family has some tough days ahead."

"No doubt about it. Let me take a look inside, just as a
precaution."

"Oh, heck," I said, patting my pockets. "Mike's got my
keys. Hang on."

I walked around the side of the house to the planter
where I hid the spare. Coming back around, I handed it to Stavlo,
who let himself in. The door swung open less than a foot and
Stavlo was drawing his weapon as quickly as only Roland Des-
chain could.

"Don't move or even breathe," he said, his gun trained on
someone in the room. Then lowering his weapon, he said, "Mike
Leigh, you've done some damn stupid things over the course of
the last twelve months, but this one just about got you killed."

"I'm sorry. Sorry," he said, more visibly shaken than he
had been in the interrogation room. Then again, looking down
the barrel of a gun will do that to most. "I'm sorry, Father. When
I arrived, the police were here. I told them who I was and they
said they were wrapping up and I could come in. Wow. What a
mess."

"Actually, not as bad as I remember," I responded, looking
around as I entered.

"Oh. I've been cleaning. Helped me keep my mind off
things, you know? Hope you don't mind?"

"Not at all, but Mike, why are you here?"

"I told Cassandra everything. Can you believe it? She already knew. Had for the last nine months she said. Anyhow, I don't think its a good idea for me to stay there right now."

"Well... I've only got the couch and Zekey Boy is going to be none to pleased about being kicked off, but your welcome to it." What else was there to do?

"I can get a hotel if its a bother."

"No. No bother," I said, without hesitating.

"I'll figure out what to do in a day or so. Promise."

"We'll work it out. Detective, I'll see you... sometime." We shook hands.

"Good night, Mike."

"Yes, sir."

WEDNESDAY 5:41 A.M.

Mike woke long before Z and I had even considered the idea. It started with a coughing fit and continued with a trip to the bathroom. By that time, Z Boy had already been up and down off the bed twice and was getting fairly insistent that he needed out. I decided it was probably time to get up when Mike stuck his head in the bedroom door.

"Hey, Father, good morning." He sounded like he had had the best night's sleep of his life. *Morning people:" what an abomination!*

"Good morning, Mike." *Happy priest person. Happy priest person...*

"Wasn't sure, is it OK to let the dog out?"

"Yeah. Just leave the door ajar. He knows his way back in."

"Nose his way back in. That's pretty funny," he said as he headed back down the hall to tend to the beast.

Huh?

Living alone - with the exception of himself - does not make one a great conversationalist before the first pot of coffee. Fortunately, my participation in this discussion was not required. Mike acted like he had been asleep all night, but apparently he had laid awake into the late hours making plans. Although I wasn't keeping track of everything, I was very pleased to understand that his number one priority was to make things right with Cassandra and the girls. He didn't have everything worked out and he knew it was probably a long shot at this point, but he was going to try.

"Janine had been something... I don't know... wonderful.

I hate to say it, but, yeah, wonderful, but she and I both knew it was wrong. And ultimately we both knew it wouldn't last. I'm going to try and make it right with her too, if I can, but no matter what, I'm determined to try and work things out with Cassandra. Janine is wonderful, but I really do love Cassandra. We just lost something along the way. Both of us," he said, trailing off on those last words. I let him think, but after a few moments, "Does that make sense, Father? Should I try or should I just walk away and let everyone get their lives back together again in whatever form that may take?"

"Mike, I'm not in full pastoral mode, not enough coffee yet...."

"I'm sorry, Father. I shouldn't be hitting you up with this so early."

"No, it's OK. What I was going to say is that as far as I can see, your marriage to Cassandra has hit bottom, which means it is going to end, unless," I said, holding up my hand to halt his protest, "unless something can change. In this case, based on what I know, I would say that you are both going to have to change - considerably - but you will never know unless you try. Mike?"

"Yeah."

"Try."

I'm not much for talking in the morning and I'm definitely not up for hugs either, but I made an exception in this case. There were tears in his eyes when he pulled back, but there was also resolve.

"I'm going to own what I did. No excuses. Then I will, Father. I will try with all that I am."

We sat silently for a while longer. When he retreated back into his own thoughts, I began to make ready for the day.

"I need to take care of the mutt and answer a few emails, so you can have the shower first, just save me a little hot water."

"Will do, Father," and he was off.

I moved his bedding to the end of the couch and the boy jumped up next to me and placed his head in my lap. This is how we spent the first part of each day, with one another, a cup of coffee and time with our God in prayer. Even Z seemed to know it was a time to be still.

After Mike had left for work, Zeke and I headed over to the church. I could see that the parking lot was empty, even Dean Harris' car had been removed. Miss Avery wasn't due back until Monday, but the entire parish was anxious for her return - *none more so than me!*

The morning passed quietly and quickly, and when it was time for the Wednesday Mass I moved through the church turning on the necessary lights and unlocking the doors. I entered the sacristy and began to vest, thinking of Dean Harris as I put on the vestments he had worn so often.

I was lost in my thoughts, but after I rang the bells and came out the side door to the altar, I was caught by surprise. We normally see twenty or so at this service, but today it was easily more than double. Folks were smiling. Folks were hungry.

Lord, help me to feed them.

"Blessed be God: Father, Son and Holy Spirit."

"And blessed be his kingdom, now and for ever. Amen."

Words so familiar to most that we scarcely needed the prayer books. So familiar, and now of all times, so very comforting.

So consumed was I in my own worship during that service that I didn't notice him until he came forward to receive communion. He knelt at the altar rail, crossed himself in a manner that only those who have been doing it all their lives know how to do reverently, and held up his hands to receive the bread.

I do not look people in the eye when I give them Holy Communion. I am only an instrument in the hands of the Lord. It is He that looks at them during this time, deep into their souls, but when I placed the bread into his hands, I could not contain my smile. Had we just gained a new member? Whatever the case, *Welcome, Thomas Stavlo.*

There was a knock at the sacristy door as I was entering the service in the church register. No surprise.

"Good afternoon, Detective," I said, without looking up.

"Padre. Got a few minutes?"

"Sorry, but if it doesn't involve lunch and coffee, I'm busy."

He held up a brown paper bag that was more covered in grease spots than not.

"Some of the finest burgers in town."

"I'll get the antacids."

We made a pot of coffee in the office kitchen and cleared enough room on my desk for a table. After shooing the beast off more than a few times, we enjoyed one of the finest and greasiest burgers I had ever eaten

"Only place I know to get a better burger is at place called Matt's Diner," Stavlo declared, wiping the remaining grease from his chin.

"Where's that?"

"Butte, Montana."

"Long ways to go for takeout."

"You've never had their burgers," he said, pulling out a stack of papers from an inside pocket. That vest of his was beginning to remind me of Hermione's beaded handbag in *Harry Potter and the Deathly Hallows*. He laid the papers in front of me.

"These are copies of the pages from the Dean's black book. As far as we can tell, there is nothing pertaining to the case in them. We wondered if you could take a look at them and let us know."

"Sure."

I read as he went for the coffee. There was nothing of interest. Mostly notes for sermons, a few names with times written out beside them, I assumed meetings, and other reminders. The only thing slightly out of place was the reference to an exceptionally good zombie movie. *Dean Harris, I never knew!*

After a few more minutes of reading I gave my report to Stavlo who had returned with coffee.

"Nothing."

"That's what I thought. Alright," he said after a moment and reaching down to scratch the Zekester on his pointy head, "I didn't tell you because I didn't want to distract you from this," he said, picking up the papers and returning them to that interior pocket, "but the team went to Janine's place last night and found it ransacked. The whole place had been tossed. There were also some indications of a struggle, spots of blood, but not enough to suggest that she had been stabbed there. Seems like someone may have been waiting for her or got in somehow, but they didn't break in. No signs of a forced entry, which means she didn't lock the door when she got home so it was probably someone she knew and let in, or they had a key. They came in, knocked her a good one, and took her somewhere else."

The phone rang and the caller ID read, "EDioc."

"Canon Bob, you're going to have to wait," I said, and let it go to voicemail. To Stavlo, "This makes no sense."

"It does to somebody and the only ones unaccounted for at this point, that we know of, are your treasurer, Hank Slidell and Elvis. Has anyone heard from Hank?"

"No."

"Alright. As for Elvis, he's pulled a real Houdini."

The phone rang again. Without looking at the caller ID and with a bit more annoyance than I should have let on, I answered "Canon Bob, I was just getting ready to call you back."

It was not Canon Bob.

"Carolyn, I'm so sorry. Crazy day around here. What can I do for you?"

I listened.

"I can be there in less than half an hour. Say, Detective Stavlo is here with me. Would it be alright if he joined me?" I asked looking up at him. "We've got to start sorting some of this out." I nodded at him, "Yes, I understand. We'll be there shortly."

"Janine has been moved out of ICU," I said, hanging up. "She wants to talk with me, but is willing to help you anyway she can. She's still weak though, so we are not to tire her out."

"Let's go get some answers."

"Yes, please."

I ran Z Man back over to the rectory and met Stavlo out front. It was a quiet ride as we both were trying to work out what we may learn.

RED DEMON

He hadn't eaten for two days and he hadn't really slept for most of the week. He was scared, his head hurt, and one of his many acquaintances had informed him that the po-lice were looking for him. He wasn't worried about the po-lice, he'd had more than his share of run-ins with them, so he knew how to handle that, but he wasn't sure that they could protect him from the Red Demon if they hauled him in. The King would know what to do, but he was still unsettled.

"Talk to me, Aaron."

Silence, except for the mice scurrying between the walls of the condemned house he had been holed up in ever since the demon had attacked him and run him off from the church.

"What kind of church let's the demons run around like that?" he asked the emptiness around him.

He wasn't sure how many days it had been, but that night he'd set up in his normal spot along the tree line next to the rock pile. (Folks over there were respectful of one another's claims and there'd be trouble if they weren't.) The church had been busy all day...

"More priests than the Pope's got tur-lets," he said, making himself laugh.

... and it was late before it was safe to move around much, but he wanted a bath down by the Menomonee, so he waited it out across the road. When most had left, he crossed over and worked his way through the tree line. He found his spot and settled in after his bath. He had had a bite to eat and was enjoying a bit of drink when he heard a car start up over at the church. Peering over the rock pile, he watched as a car went careening out of the lot.

"There's one for the po-lice," he said.

He turned in time to see the new priest running back into the church. No sooner had the door closed when the Red Demon came running out from behind the church and headed directly for him.

He'd thought it was just a man at first, but he saw as the demon passed under the closest streetlamp that it was all red, grinning like a banshee with wild eyes. He'd never forget that face.

When the demon got too close, he jumped up. The demon stopped just a few steps in front of him, but then with a silent scream, charged. He raised his hands to ward off any blows, he didn't want to be possessed by this one, but he still took a mighty blow to the head, which put him on the ground.

The demon pounced on him and delivered several more hits, but these didn't seem to be so hard, no worse than getting hit by one of those punks in those packs of kids that roamed the streets looking to prove their 'manhood' by beating up the helpless. The demon then started rustling around him, cursing under his breath. Kept saying, "Where is it?"

"Sounded like a man, to tell the truth."

Elvis had thought about answering and telling him he didn't have it, but Aaron told him to shut up and lie still. He did, not even grunting when the demon kicked him in the ribs.

Then it was gone, but it was still several minutes before he dared allow himself to move, and then only the shallowest of breaths. When he could no longer hear the demon crashing through the trees...

"I'd thought they all could fly."

... he quickly gathered up his few belongings and ran, sticking close to the trees, which turned out to be a good thing. If he had been out in the open the po-lice would have spotted him when they came up all flashy-flashy.

He walked all night and didn't enter the rundown house he was now in until near dawn. He had wanted to get as far from the Red Demon as possible.

Since then, he'd only ventured out once for supplies, but he would have to go again today.

"Before dark and before that red bastard comes out for the night! That's for sure."

WEDNESDAY 2:18 P.M.

Carolyn met us in the hall outside of Janine's room. She had been moved to room 384, which indicated to me, based on my previous visits and patient status, that she was doing well. Stavlo and I must have had the looks of two crusaders convinced they had discovered the Holy Grail as we approached the door, because Carolyn, who happened to be standing outside the door talking on her cellphone, held up her hand with arm fully extended like a school crossing guard in a fluorescent green vest.

"Hold on there boys," she said after hanging up, eyeing us both as only a mother could. "She is out of the woods, but she still needs plenty of rest. Over do it and I'll call the nurse."

We understood, but she followed us in just the same.

"Father, Anthony," Janine said, looking much better than she had yesterday. "So good to see you. I'm sorry," she said, rubbing her forehead and looking at Stavlo, "I can't remember your name."

"Detective Thomas Stavlo, ma'am."

"Oh my. Do I look so bad you call me ma'am?"

"Not at all," we chimed in together.

The pleasantries continue for a few minutes, but then it was Janine who decided that it was time to get on with it.

"Mom, I don't want this to sound rude, but I need to talk with Father Anthony and Detective...."

"Stavlo."

"Stavlo, alone for a while. I'll have one of them find you when we're done."

"Don't overdo," she said, looking uncertain. "Father."

"Yes, ma'am."

She only gave me a look and I was instantly more afraid of her than I was of the nurse from the night before.

"Yes, ma'am," I said again to confirm my understanding.

As with Mike, there was going to be no rushing Janine. She would tell her story and give her confession. Stavlo and I settled in on either side of her bed. There were no tears from Janine. She was strong.

"Father, I'm planning on coming to you for confession as soon as I'm able, but this is going to have to do for now."

"It'll be just fine."

"And detective," she said, turning to him, "I know you're going to press me for details, but I have to tell you right up front that a lot of what has happened is still a blur. I keep trying to remember, but it won't come."

"I understand."

She paused, gathering her thoughts.

"You said you knew," she began, "about Mike and I?"

I nodded.

"I've been told that I'm 'pretty' enough times to realize there is a certain amount of truth to it, but I have to tell you, the pretty girls, at least in my case, don't get too many dates. Seems the guys look at a pretty girly, ogle her or whatever, but they never think of asking us out. I guess they think we have more dates than we can handle, but not me, so when Mike began to pay me a little bit of attention, well... I was flattered, then I fell in love.

"That night we were at the Chapter dinner at his house, Cassandra... my goodness, you see folks in church and talk to them, then you see them outside of the pews and... well.... wow. I pray that if I'm ever married, I never even think of treating my husband in such a way. In private or otherwise. It was really awful. I know he's got his faults, but I sat there watching him as she heaped on the insults, I couldn't help but wondering what kind of man he would be if someone loved him just a little. Turns out, I discovered he is an amazing man.

"Father, I wasn't trying to break up a marriage. I wasn't

trying to do anything. I just found, for the first time in my life, someone who made me truly happy. Someone I looked forward to seeing or at least hearing from each day."

Shut up. Shut up. Shut up. Let her talk.

"And I knew it was wrong. We both knew it was wrong, but I didn't have the will power to quit. It was only when I knew what we were planning on the night the Dean was murdered that I realized Mike did. He's a better person than I am. Much better. Even while we were... I don't even know what to call it... Dating?... He would talk about his girls and even about Cassandra. He would tell me that he loved them and I never doubted him. Loving his wife, I don't know where I thought our relationship was going, but I just kept hanging on. Ten percent of something is better than ten percent of nothing. You know what I mean?"

"Yeah," Stavlo said quietly, causing both Janine and I to jump. I guess we had forgotten he was there for a moment.

"Yeah," she said, looking in his eyes and possibly seeing a kinsman. "That night I knew what was coming and I wanted it to be special.

"Father," she reached out and took my hand, "I know what I'm talking about is sinful. It's terrible what I did, but I won't say that Mike didn't make me happy or that I regret it."

The story tells of a WWII priest who would go to the soldiers on the front line and ask if they wanted to make confession. Some would say yes and others no. The priest remembers one in particular who confessed many sins involving wine and women. He then asked the young man, "Are you sorry for these sins?" The young man gave it a good hard think and then responded, "Father, honestly I'm not. I loved all those women and the wine was good." The priest, knowing that the young man may or may not even survive the day did not want to send him off without absolution, so after a moments thought asked, "Well, then, are you sorry that you are not sorry?" The young soldier responded, "Oh, gosh, Father, I certainly am!" Making the sign of the cross over the young soldier, the priest said, "Dominus noster Jesus Christus te absolvat; et ego...."

We all have to start somewhere.

"Keep going. Tell us the story."

She looked over at Stavlo, probably to see how he was judging her. He nodded in understanding, so she continued.

"The night started in the toilet and went down from there. I had to work late. My boss, Hank Sli...."

"Where is he?" Stavlo stopped her and asked.

"Um.. the last time I heard from him, he was heading down to his mom's place in Kansas."

"Do you know why?"

"Late Wednesday afternoon, about the time we were heading out, he came in to tell me that he was taking the next flight out to Kansas City. His sister called and told him that their mom had had a stroke. Haven't you heard from him," she asked, looking to me.

"No."

"I... I was supposed to let the folks at the office know, then... what a mess."

Stavlo leaned back in his chair. Another suspect with an alibi. Outside of Mike and Elvis, there were no other real leads.

"Do you know what town his mother lives in?"

She smiled. "Leavenworth."

"Give me a minute," he said, standing and walked outside the room.

When he was out of earshot.

"How's Mike?"

"He's a mess, but you should know, he's going to work on saving his family. He seems quite determined."

"Good," she said thoughtfully.

"Will you respect that?"

"You mean, will I stop playing the home wrecker?"

"I never said or implied anything like that."

"I know. It's just how I think of myself." A short pause, "Yes. I will do whatever is necessary to help them."

I nodded.

"I mean this kindly, but the best thing you can do is help

Mike keep his vows by staying clear."

She nodded.

"I can do that."

At that moment, I knew she would and could.

"Keep going," Stavlo said, stepping back into the room and taking his seat.

"Well, I had to work late and didn't get to the hotel until much later than I had planned. By the time I got there, Mike had started drinking and had already put away a few scotches. He's got to ease up. So, instead of going out for dinner, we went up to the room. We laughed and we cried. It was over. But then he began to tell me about his visit to see Dean Harris. I was so furious. He had no right.

"He told me that in the course of resigning as the President of the chapter that he ended up making a full confession and gave Dean Harris my name. I didn't really know what to think, but that just seemed so awful. I felt so much shame, wondering what Dean Harris thought of me.

"I tried to get more out of Mike about what was said and what Dean Harris had said, but by then he was over his limit. He started reminiscing about our time together, talking about his girls and how proud he was of them, all sorts of things. When I asked him again what had been said, he responded with a snore.

"I knew the funeral for the bishop had taken place that day and that the Dean would be at the church. It wasn't that late and I thought I just might be able to catch him. My gas light had come on in my car several miles before I got to the hotel, so I...."

"Took Mike's car," Stavlo said, nodding.

"Yeah," she said, a bit surprised that he would know that. "I took Mike's car and drove to the church. It took about half an hour to get there, but when I arrived there were still several cars around. I pulled into to the staff parking lot, saw that the Dean's car was still there, and parked in Mike's place.

"When I entered the building, I took the east cloister so that I maybe wouldn't run into anyone coming out of the Parish Hall. As I came to the crossway to the cloister, I saw Dean

Harris walking by in the west cloister, but then I got scared, so I went into the women's bathroom and hid in one of the stalls for awhile."

"Did you see or hear anyone," Stavlo asked.

"Other than the Dean, no. At least, not yet."

He nodded.

"By the time I got my nerve again, they were already turning out the lights. Someone came in, wiggled the handle on one of the toilets that was running, and turned off the lights on the way out."

"That was me," I said, looking apologetically.

"When I came out of the bathroom, I had decided to forget it and just leave, but I turned to the west cloister instead. It felt like everyone was gone by then, but then I heard the Dean's voice in the sanctuary. Were you," she said, looking at me a bit uncertainly, "were you in St. Mary's Courtyard."

"I was."

"She's so beautiful..." She trailed off.

"Janine?" Stavlo wasn't impatient, but he needed answers.

"Sorry. I saw you, then there was a yell and a crash. It was horrible, so out of place."

"Do you know who yelled?"

"I only know it wasn't the Dean. I couldn't hear what he was saying, but I could hear the Dean's voice. So kind. Even then. So kind. Then the yell and the crash. I was scared and didn't move. I turned to go, but then decided that the Dean might be sick and need help, so I walked to the sanctuary. Only the lights in the front were on and the Dean was alone, sitting in the Bishop's chair.

BLOOD ON MY FACE

Janine stood at the cloister entrance into the sanctuary looking for whoever else had been speaking, but there was no one in sight. She saw that both doors to the sacristy were open, but it didn't appear that anyone was in there. Walking up the aisle she called to the Dean.

"Dean Harris."

He stirred a little, but did not turn. She then saw his hand slide from his chest.

"Dean Harris," she called again, picking up her pace as she went forward, fearing now that the Dean was ill. "Dean Harris? Oh my God."

She came up short when she saw the blood. So much blood. She didn't understand how, but it seemed to be pumping straight out of his chest. She ran to him, careful not to step in the blood on the floor.

"Dean, what happened?"

She reached out to press on the wound in his chest, only then realizing that something was protruding from it. She had seen it before, but could not place what it was. She had no idea what to do, so instinctively she placed her hand down where she believed the wound was, but that did nothing to stop the flow of blood.

The Dean opened his eyes and stared directly into Janine's. She could almost sense a smile in them, then a streak of pain crossed his face and the smile faded and the life ended.

Janine had never witnessed death, but without even knowing it, her soul had taken a dramatic turn.

"Dean. Dean Harris," she said, shaking him. "Oh God." She

reached up and touched her mouth with the hand that had been pressing against the Dean's chest, unaware that she had covered the lower part of her face in the Dean's blood.

A noise behind her. She turned, but there was no one. Only then did she realize the danger that she might be in. This was no accident. Someone had done this to him. Another noise, further off in the dark of the nave.

"Who's there?" she called. "Hello?"

Darkness and silence, but a feeling. Someone was watching.

She made her way down the steps and tried to look further into the nave, but it was too dark. Rounding the corner, she looked into the sacristy, but there was no one. She went in, not remembering if there was, but hoping to hide from the hidden watcher and praying for a phone to call for help. There wasn't. Just as she was about to go out the secondary door into the sanctuary and back to the Dean, she heard someone whistling - *I Have Confidence.* It was Father Anthony.

"Excuse me, Sir," Father Anthony called. Much closer now.

Janine panicked. She remembered the under-passage and turned for the door. On the small counter beside the door they kept the red church register book, where the clergy recorded all the services, date, time, attendance, etc. Dean Harris must have been filling in the information on the Bishop's funeral, because there beside it was his little black book. Everyone in the parish knows about that little black book and everyone in the parish knows he was constantly making notes in it. On impulse she grabbed it, fearing that her name might be one of those notes.

"Excuse me," Father Anthony calls. He was so close that she thought he was speaking to her. No. He's still in the sanctuary.

Quickly opening the under-passage door she ducks in. Reaching out her other hand to steady herself in the dark and unintentionally smearing blood on the wall.

"Sir!" Father Anthony called again just as the door to the

under-passage quietly closed.

She had only been down here twice and that was twice too many. Now, without the lights, she didn't dare turn them on, it was much worse. Placing one hand on the wall and one out in front of her she worked her way through. She didn't remember it being such a long ways. She thought she heard something in front of her and froze, her breath coming in short pants.

"Move," she whispered to herself. "Move." And she did.

Making another turn to the left, she stumbled over something in the passage. A step. She had reached the steps leading up. Climbing quietly and reaching the top she opened the first door, closed it, then opened the door an inch that leads into the sanctuary. She heard nothing, but could not see the altar from her position.

Run.

The instant she let go of the door, she knew her mistake. The spring slammed the door close.

Run. And she did.

As she rounded the corner with the staff parking off the side, she heard footsteps enter the cloister.

I'll never make it. But she did.

Why her pursuer hadn't followed her, she did not know. She sped out of the parking lot, only breaking briefly to turn out onto the street in front of the church. She didn't dare slow down until she was several blocks away.

Soon afterwards, she was shaking so uncontrollably, she had to pull over. Finding a side street, she came to a stop. The tears arrived along with the purging of the adrenaline. She quickly opened the door and with out getting out of the car, leaned over towards the street, and was sick. There was no tissue in the car, so she used the sleeve of her shirt to wipe her mouth and was shocked to see it now streaked with blood. Looking up into the rearview mirror, with the aid of the dim streetlights, she could see in the rearview mirror that her face was smeared with blood.

"Oh, Dean Harris, what happened? What happened?"

WEDNESDAY 3:02 P.M.

"I wiped off as much blood as I could, then went home. I pulled into the garage and went to work on the car. Cleaning it as best I could. After that I went in and took a shower."

"Why didn't you just come forward?" I asked.

"Father, I honestly don't know. I was feeling guilty. Guilty about Mike. Guilty about who I had become. Just guilty. I didn't kill Dean Harris," she said, looking over to Stavlo, "but I still felt guilty. Everyday I kept telling myself to go to the police, but then when there was nothing happening, and I couldn't add anything... I don't know. I really don't, but then on Wednesday I woke up and put my big girl pants on. I fully intended to come in, but the day just kept slipping by and then... I woke up here."

"On the night of the murder, you say you went in and took a shower, what did you do after that?" Stavlo asked.

"Well, I drove back to the hotel Mike and I were staying at. Somewhere along the way I stopped and pitched my clothes and the cleaning supplies. When I arrived at the hotel, someone else had taken the parking place Mike had been in, so I just parked as close as I could. I went upstairs, but Mike was still sleeping in the chair, so I put his keys with his other things and just left."

"What about the Dean's black book?"

"I lost it. I looked everywhere for it, but couldn't find it. I either dropped it somewhere or accidentally threw it away with my clothes and the cleaning supplies."

"Did you look in it?"

"No."

Stavlo looked up at me. His expression was clear: don't you say a word junior detective. I didn't.

"Alright. What happened the day you were attacked?"

"I went to work and I remember coming home. I was a little later than normal, but when I got home I remember turning on the TV and changing, but after that… I just can't remember," she said, shaking her head.

"There was no sign of a forced entry at your house. Do you remember locking the door when you came in? Did someone come in after you?"

"I suppose someone could have, but I've been so scared ever since the murder, so I'm always checking the locks."

"Perhaps someone came over. Knocked or rang the doorbell?"

"I don't think so, but… I don't know."

His phone beeped.

"They found Hank," he said, looking up after reading a text message. "He's at his mom's. Said that he was in such hurry to get home that he forgot his phone. He's fine."

It beeped again.

"His mom's got some PT to go through, but she's fine too… if you're interested."

There was silence and then there wasn't.

"Damnit!" Stavlo said, standing and pacing to the other end of the room. "This just doesn't make any damn sense!"

That little outburst brought on the ire of Carolyn who was quickly back in the room.

"Gentlemen," she said, the tone of her voice not necessarily reflecting any sincerity in referring to us a such, "I think that will be enough for the day."

"Sorry." Contrite Stavlo contained less sincerity than angry momma.

"It's OK, mom."

"No," I said, "she's right. You given us enough for now. You need some rest."

I looked to Stavlo for confirmation and he nodded reluctantly.

"Let me say a prayer with you before we go."

"Thank you, Father."

Three of us joined hands and prayed. Stavlo had made it to mass, but this was just a touch out of his comfort zone for now, although he did add his own 'Amen.'

"I'll be back to see you."

"Thank you, Father. Thank you, Detective."

"Yes, ma'am. If you think of anything else," he said, leaning over and placing his card on her nightstand, "you give me a call."

"I will," but she called him back as we were walking out. "Detective?"

"Yes."

"Am I in trouble?"

"Yes," he said without hesitation, "but you and Mike can probably split the cost of the same half-pint lawyer and both be OK in the end as long as the half-pint lawyer isn't too much of an idiot."

"Thank you."

"Yes, ma'am," he said, and tipped his imaginary hat.

She smiled.

Momma frowned.

We rode the elevator down in silence. When the electronic voice informed us that we were on the first floor, I turned to Stavlo.

"He didn't do it."

"Mike?"

"Yeah."

"No, Mike didn't do it and neither did Janine, but Dean Harris sure as hell didn't stab himself in the heart with that...."

"Fistula."

"Yeah. Fistula. Ya'know, you all could save the world a serious amount of time if you called a thing a thing instead of all this church speak," he said, storming out as soon as the elevator doors had opened. "Save people a lot of time."

Um. Yes. We get that a lot.

By the time I caught up, he was already sitting in the car with the engine running.

"The way I see it," he began, "is that I've got one solid suspect."

"Who?" I asked surprised, thinking I knew all the ins and outs.

"You," he said, without hesitation and in all seriousness. "I've got one dead priest and three other individuals attacked. I've got an illicit affair, an absentee treasurer, and a homeless fella who thinks he's Elvis. The only common denominator is you," he said, turning to me as though looking for an explanation.

"Oh."

"Padre, you have the right to remain silent. Anything you say can and will be used against you...." He smiled. "Who am I kidding? That goofy poodle of yours is more likely to have done it than you."

"That wasn't funny."

"Point of view, Padre. Point of view."

"You know I can excommunicate you, don't you?"

"You wouldn't," he said without a hint of worry as he put the car in reverse.

"You think not?"

"Miss Avery would be mad if you did."

"Shi...."

"Language, Padre! Don't make me tell on you."

"How did you get her to like you so quickly? Do you know how hard I've tried? I'm afraid I'm going to be assigned to St. Swithin's in the Swamp because she's going to give me such a bad recommendation."

"Collar doesn't get you everything, I see," he said, with a bark of laughter.

"Apparently not."

We managed to make it back to the rectory without insulting each other too much more. As we came into the church yard, I saw that my car and Mike's car were both in front of my house.

"You've got company."

"Not surprised."

Stopping in the drive, he put it in park and turned to face me.

"If it had only been the Dean that has been attacked we would probably be looking at something random, but there is reason behind all this. I still want to talk to him, but all the subsequent attacks and break-ins pretty much eliminate Elvis. If Janine's statement checks out...," he trailed off and was silent for several minutes.

I let him think.

"Well, Padre, ask the Man Upstairs for some divine intervention, because I've got bupkis," he said, throwing up his hands.

"Are you giving up?"

"Father, I'll go to my grave before I give up on this one or any other case I've been assigned. Somewhere along the way, he or she has made a mistake. We just haven't found it yet. Tomorrow we start from the beginning and go through it all again."

We both looked up as Mike stepped out the front door and waved and Z bounded out toward the car, putting his feet up on the driver's side window. Stavlo rolled it down to pet him.

Waving to Mike, I asked, "Can I let him know he's off the radar?"

"Why not," he said with a shrug. "Someone should have a good night."

"No doubt." Mike approached the car. Rolling down my window, I said, "Hey, Mike."

"How is she," he blurted out before I had the window rolled down.

"She's going to be fine. I'll fill you in."

"Father," completely exasperated, "how...."

"Mike. Breathe."

He did.

"I'm making supper. Care to join us," he asked after a moment, looking across to Stavlo.

"Thanks, but I've got to run."

"Ok. Well if you change your mind, I'm a pretty good cook. I'll fatten the Reverend up he said, patting me on the shoulder before walking back toward the house.

"I didn't know he was going to be here long enough to fatten me up," I said, getting out of the car.

Before backing out, he leaned over the console and said, "Shouldn't take much. From the looks of things, I'd say you're almost there."

"Huh? What?"

I could still hear him laughing as he drove away.

If he stayed long, he would fatten me up. It was the finest meal cooked in the rectory since I had moved in. When he heard that he was off the hook, he tried to bolt for the hospital, but I reminded him of what Stavlo had said and that Janine needed rest, *not to mention, Momma was more likely to let an armored division roll through the room before she allowed Mike in.*

When the meal was over, we cleared the dishes and Mike chatted. Cassandra wouldn't speak to him, but the girls came out while he was there. They had run up and hugged him. He thought Cassandra's face had softened at seeing this, but when she caught him looking at her she hardened up again.

"Go slow, Mike. It took a long time for your marriage to get in this condition and so it won't be fixed over night. There's a lot of trust that's been lost that must be restored before you all can make any progress. Slow."

"Yes, but it was hopeful."

The phone rang.

"Tony."

Bob!

"Canon Bob, good evening."

"Tony, I know we can't force you to, but you really should consider getting a mobile."

Too much time watching BBC.

"Yes, sir."

"Are you available Friday afternoon around 2:00 p.m. I'd like to stop by and get an update on what's taking place. This business is taking far too long to sort out."

"Friday is my day off...."

"So you'll be free. Good. And see if you can have that police person there as well, better yet, see if you can have his superior there. At this point, I think we need to put a bit of pressure on."

"Canon Bob, I can assure you that...."

"I'm sorry, Tony, I've got other diocesan business to work through before I'm able to call it a day. Two o'clock Friday."

"Yes...."

Click.

"... you pretentious... oh, never mind," I said to the receiver and hung up.

"What's that," Mike asked, coming in from the kitchen.

I just shook my head.

"Maybe this will make you feel better."

"What's this?" It was hard to tell underneath the mountain whip cream.

"Cherry pie."

Maybe Z will help me out.

THURSDAY 10:00 A.M.

"I am resurrection and I am Life, says the Lord. Whoever has faith in me shall have life, even though he die...."

The congregation stood and the Paschal Candle led the family and I up the aisle.

Too many funerals and this one for Reese was as hard on the parish as was the Dean's. We had been with her when her children were born and watched them grow as a family. In them we saw the hope of many lived out, but then a single cell in her body, a bit like that one piece of fruit in the garden, changed the course forever. However, the light of the Paschal Candle was a reminder that darkness does not win. And so we mourned as a family, but we also rejoiced in a greater hope.

The reception afterwards was difficult on Daniel and the girls as person after person came up to them and told them how special Reese was to them. If their grief were even a fraction of the family's, it would have been severe. What came through clearly was that Daniel would not have to raise his girls alone. He had a family consisting of grandmothers and grandfathers, aunts and uncles, nieces and nephews, and more cousins than you could count. That family was not related to him through blood, but they were related to him through Christ and St. Matthew's and they would be as loyal as any blood relations. That was something the Payne family could count on, and God help the boys that tried to date the girls when they grew up.

Not wanting to draw folks from the family, but out of a sincere love for Reese, Miss Avery also came for the reception, escorted by her sister. Her presence brought even more light to that day.

"Miss Avery," I said, pulling up a chair and sitting next to her after the line of well-wishers had diminished, "what a blessing to have you today."

"Oh, Father Anthony," she began, wiping a tear from her cheek, "my sister wouldn't allow me to come to the funeral, said it would be too emotional, but I had to come and pay my respects. Such a dear family."

"Yes. We'll help them through. That's what we do," I said, taking her hand, as much for my comfort as for hers. "You are feeling better?"

"Much. Thank you." With a look of absolute determination, she added, "I will - whether my sister approves or not - I will be back to work on Monday, even if only for half a day. There must be so much to do!"

"Many of the members are trying to keep things moving, but without you and Jimmy...."

"Oh, sorry Father, how is Jimmy?"

"He got to go home yesterday. Looking really good. Nancy'll take good care of him."

Miss Avery glanced at me over the top of her glasses as if to say otherwise.

"He's going to be fine."

"Yes. Yes he will. Oh, Father, I'll be so glad when things get back to normal. This really has been too much."

"Yes it has."

Normal would be good.

When Daniel was free for a moment, he brought the girls over to say "Hello" to Miss Avery. I moved away and let them have their time together.

Normal would be very good.

I glanced around to make sure that everything was as it should be, then stepped out and found myself once again in St. Mary's Courtyard.

I spent the next hour before our Lady, not praying, but retracing the last week and a half that seemed like much more time than that. The one conclusion that I came to was that no matter the outcome, no matter if we discovered the culprit and their motives, none of this was going to make any sense. Perhaps I live too sheltered of a life. Perhaps this was just evil. And in the midst of it all, we are to discover God.

"You know, at the moment, we could use a bit of the water into wine," I said to Our Lady.

Silence. Silence, but peace.

Peace I can live with.

The door leading into the courtyard gave a soft squeak.

"Sorry to disturb you, Father," Mike said from the steps leading down, "but Detective Stavlo is on the phone. It didn't seem urgent. Would you like for me to have him call back later?"

"No. I'll come." Turning back to Our Lady, I smiled. "Thank you for helping me find what I was looking for."

As I walked to the office, passing Mike as he held the door for me and some of the other members of the congregation who were cleaning up after the reception who looked at me and smiled or nodded, I realized something: I would never be allowed to stay on as the Dean of St. Matthew's, but I was no longer the curate. I had been allowed to become a leader of this congregation. Of this family.

"Padre. Knew you had a busy day, but thought I should check-in. All's well?"

"Honestly," I said, closing the door to my office, "even with everything going on, it seemed like one of the most normal days we've had around here since the Bishop died. You?"

"Can't complain, but other than Elvis - and he's not likely our killer - we've no more to go on. Hank Slidell is supposed to be back in town tonight and he's willingly agreed to come in and visit with me first thing tomorrow. I'm not expecting any leads, but its just one of the loose ends that needs clearing up..."

OTHER LOOSE ENDS

"If she remembers anything that happened, we're done."

"I know that."

"Well, you're not acting like it."

"Hey, it was your guy that was supposed to take care of her. How the hell did he mess that up? Have you been able to reach him?"

"No. He's not answering."

"Call him again."

"It's been less that ten minutes since I tried."

"So."

The number was dialed.

"Put it on speaker."

They stared intently at the phone as it rang, as though that would convince the other party to answer. It did.

"Look. I know you two want to talk to me, but I'm busy. You're not the only people I have jobs for, so...."

"You didn't finish our job!"

"What do you mean I didn't finish your job! The only thing in that girl's future was a toe tag."

"Well you can tell her that yourself, because she is presently recovering nicely at St. Anthony's Hospital and I'm guessing she's explaining everything to the police as we speak."

"That's not possible."

"Clearly it is."

"You need to finish the job!"

"Damnit," he whispered. "Fine. What room is she in?"

"384."

He hung up.

"Where did you find this guy?"

"The internet. Where else?"

"For crying out loud, on the internet, five bucks and an email address will buy you a Ph.d. in physics."

"Well then, I should have gotten a whole lot more for the $1,500 I spent."

"I'm not going down for his screwup."

"And you think I am."

Silence.

"I gotta go to work."

"I need the car."

"Then you'll just have to give me a ride, won't ya?"

"Fine. When's your's getting out of the shop, anyhow?"

"As soon as I can pay for the repairs."

THURSDAY 2:07 P.M.

"...anyhow," Stavlo continued, "my daughter is coming over for supper."

"Your daughter?"

"Yes. Daughter. I say she's coming over for supper, but she's actually coming over to make supper. She's the chef at one of the downtown restaurants. I never know what she's going to serve, but I've never been disappointed. Care to join us?"

"I made him an offer he couldn't refuse," I said in my best *Godfather* impression. "Time?"

"Make it six."

"Deal."

He gave me the address then hung up.

"Daughter?" I was saying to myself as I came out of my closet only to discover Miss Avery sitting at her desk. "You are not supposed to be here."

"Father Anthony, how could it stack up so fast," Miss Avery said, completely distraught. "It will take weeks to clear this all up."

"It can take until next year for all I care, but that doesn't change the fact that you are not supposed to be here."

"I'll second that! Janis," Miss Avery's sister said, standing in the doorway, hands on hips. "You promised!"

"I know," she said, tears welling up, "but I just feel so useless, sitting around all day reading or watching that stupid TV. This is where I belong."

"Yes, it is where you belong," I said, taking her by the arm and helping her stand. "It is where you belong on Monday, but not until."

"Father Anthony, I saw what the bulletins looked like for this past Sunday. A travesty," she whispered, fearing the one who produced those bulletins might overhear. I did. "I could at least put one in proper order."

"You can...."

"...on Monday," her sister and I said together.

"You two!" She tried not to smile.

"Yes," her sister said, taking her free hand, "we two love you and care about you."

"Fine. Fine, but Father, be sure and look over the bulletin before letting them send one out like that again. It's a reflection on me," she said, putting her hand to her chest.

"Promise."

The two chittered, chattered, and bickered all the way down the hall, but they were happy to have one another.

Turning back toward the office.

"Ho! Dang, Mike. Scared the daylights out of me."

"Sorry, Father. Sorry. Say, I'm the last one here. Thought I'd lock up before heading back to the office. You need anything?"

"No. I'm good. A little catching up is all."

"Ok. See you tonight for supper."

"Sounds good... no. Wait. I've got to go out tonight. I'll be home a bit late. You go ahead."

"Right. Mr. Zeke and I'll be bachelors tonight," he said, waving as he went. I heard the door catch and lock behind him, but after only a few minutes alone in the building, I got up and rechecked every door.

Standing in the sanctuary, with the light coming through the stained glass windows and the sanctuary lamp burning up by the altar, I wondered how someone could come into such a place and commit such a crime.

"Hm. I guess the church has been committing crimes for 2,000 years. Perhaps we're overdo."

Lord, help me, if I'm already becoming a cynic.

"That's not supposed to happen for another two

months," I said, heading back to my closet.

The phone rang a few times, but the caller ID indicated it was only 800 numbers, so I was able to spend three uninterrupted hours studying and preparing the Sunday sermon. I wasn't at all surprised when the Gospel lesson was the calming of the storm. I... we had a lot to work from on that one.

I walked through the front door and my knees nearly buckled. He must have known from the expression on my face.

"I told you. She's one heck of a cook. Molly," he said, turning to the beautiful young woman in the kitchen, "Molly, meet The Reverend Anthony Savel, a.k.a. Padre. Padre, Molly Stavlo, a.k.a. I-make-Emeril-Lagasse-look-like-a-second-hand-hash-slinger."

"Delighted to meet you," I said, extending a hand.

"Same," she said, while looking at her father as though he were the idiot she always thought he was when she was sixteen.

"Come on in, Padre. Did you bring Zeke?"

"Um, no."

"Oh." He was truly disappointed. "I've been telling Molly all about him. Next time, he comes."

"I'll let him know."

"What'll you have? Beer, scotch, water?"

I was pleased with the work I had accomplished today and Canon Bob was coming tomorrow.

"Scotch."

"That a boy. Molly," he said, marching into the kitchen, "we're having a party."

"Dad," she said, turning to him, "you...."

She stopped. Cocked her head and smiled.

"You, I love."

He took his daughter by the hand and danced her around the kitchen to a tune that only he could hear, but must have been even more amazing than anything the greatest composers had ever written.

"How much have you had to drink," she asked, when he

finally let her get back to cooking.

"Nine cups of coffee and...," picking up a large cup with a straw and sucking until it gurgled, "... forty-eight ounces of pure water. I believe I'll have a brew."

She only shook her head.

The meal was exquisite and the conversation even more so. Molly was very different from her father, but there was definitely some of him in her.

"There were suppose to be leftovers," Molly said, gazing into an empty dish. "For like two days."

Stavlo and I cheersed our decaf coffees.

"I knew we could do it, if we put our minds to it," he said.

It seemed to be about the right time for me to be heading home. When Stavlo's phone rang, I stood with him and made ready.

He grimaced then answered.

"Stavlo."

A short pause.

"What!"

Another short pause.

"Oh, for shi...," he cut himself off and hung up. "We have to go."

"No problem," I said. Looking to Molly, "I can let myself out...."

"Not Molly and I. You and I. I love you, sweetheart," he said, kissing her quickly on the cheek. "Sorry."

"I may be here when you get back, if that is OK?"

"Of course it is. *Mi casa. Su casa,* just don't steal anything."

She laughed, in spite of the fact that she had probably heard that same line all her life.

"Ok, bye," I said, reaching out for a quick handshake. "Truly a pleasure and the meal...." I reached out and grabbed the last roll off the plate and made a quick dip in the last of the gravy. "Umm!"

"That was mine," he said, grabbing his keys off the bar

and heading for the door.

"Um hu mun nuw."

He didn't start talking until we were underway.

"Someone attacked Janine. In the hospital!"

"What? Who?"

"Hopefully we'll have some answer... No. We damn well better have some answers when we get there."

I let him focus on driving. At this rate of speed, with the lights of his unmarked car flashing all around us and clearing most of the traffic as we went, I thought it best.

We were greeted on the third floor by a hallway full of police.

"What the...?"

"Boss." I recognized the young detective hurrying up to Stavlo. It was Riley.

"Where the hell were you?"

"There were two nurses outside her room and I had to use the restroom. Three minutes tops!" He and I were both hurrying along at Stavlo's heels, trying to keep up. The hallway full of police parted as we... he came through.

"Three minutes too long," he growled.

As they turned the corner toward Janine's room, there were more police standing around and one man in dark clothes lying on the ground facedown with his hands cuffed behind his back. There was a bloody patch of hair on the back of his head.

"Who's he?"

"He won't say, but his ID says he is one Fred Riner. We're running it."

"Who gave him that?" Stavlo asked, pointing at the back of Riner's head.

"I did."

Carolyn stood in the doorway of her daughters room, looking somewhat shaken, but also more than willing to clout anyone else who thought they were getting in.

"Father," she said, "please thank the church for sending

that nice bouquet of flowers with the heavy vase. It's busted, but it came in handy."

"I'll be sure and pass that along, Carolyn, but what happened?"

"You two can come in, but do not upset my daughter anymore than she is."

Her tone indicated that she would find another vase if we did.

"Father," Janine frantically called when she saw me. "What have I done? I don't understand any of this."

"That's what we're here to figure out," Stavlo answered, coming up behind me. "What do you remember?"

"I remember dying," she said quietly. "Mom saved...." Then she began to cry.

"It's OK. It's OK, Sugapop," Carolyn whispered, wiping her daughters forehead and pushing her hair back. "It's OK."

"Carolyn, I know this is a difficult situation, but what can you tell me."

She looked at Janine who nodded.

"We were both tired, so we called it an early evening. I was sleeping in the chair over in the corner." She indicated the spot where she had been on the evening I had first met her. "The nurses come and go, so when I saw someone enter, I assumed it was a nurse, but then I heard Janine. She was struggling. I turned on this little pen light I've been carrying and there he was."

The shock of what she had seen happening to her daughter was setting in. Her voice broke.

"He had a pillow over her face," she said, putting her hand to her mouth, holding back the breakdown. "She was flailing her arms, trying to get him off, but she's still too weak to fight off someone like that.

"When I turned on the flashlight, it startled him and he turned to run." She was looking toward the door. "I don't even recall thinking about it. I picked up that vase of flowers and threw it as hard as I could. We were state softball champs when I was in high school," she said, laughing through her distress.

"You've still got it," Stavlo said.

"If you want to put me in jail for it you can. I don't care."

"Put you in jail? No. Give you a medal? Probably."

"Oh."

"Janine, if I get a picture of this guy's face, could you tell me who he is?"

"If I know him, yes."

"Riley," he barked.

He rushed in.

"Yes, sir?"

"Do you think you could get a picture of his mug without messing that up?"

"Done," Riley said, looking for anything to get back on the boss' good side.

"Make it quick."

We all waited.

"Take your time," Stavlo said, walking over the door. Riley ran into him.

"Sorry," he said, handing his cell phone over to Stavlo who frowned.

"He's awake and he wouldn't hold still."

Stavlo only shook his head as he walked to the side of the bed and held the phone down so that Janine could see.

She studied his face, but there was no sign of recognition.

"I've honestly never seen him before."

He held the phone up to me. I shook my head. He pitched the phone back to Riley.

"Get his prints. See if they match up to anything we found at Janine's place."

"Yes, sir."

Riley didn't move.

"What exactly are you waiting for?"

"Right. Nothing sir. Yes, sir."

"Like a greyhound, that one," he said sarcastically, turning back to Janine and Carolyn.

"Janine, everyone has enemies, but it takes a particular

sort of enemy to send someone to try and kill you."

"Detective," I said, perhaps not wanting him to startle her too badly.

He frowned again.

"Yeah," he said and nodded. "Janine, is there anyone? Anything? That would bring someone to do this?"

She thought.

"The only person who might be this angry with me is Cassandra, but I don't even know that she knows who I am."

"Cassandra, who's that?" Carolyn asked.

Janine took a deep breath.

"The wife of the man I had an affair with."

"Oh, Janine." Hand to her mouth again.

"Not so much a sugapop anymore, am I, mom?"

"You'll always be my, Sugapop," Carolyn said, throwing her arms around her daughter. "No matter what. You'll always be."

They held each other.

"Come on, Padre," he said, and motioned for me to follow.

Riley almost ran into him again as we walked out of the room. He stepped aside, but kept in step as we walked back toward the elevator.

"Make sure no one goes into that room without a police escort. I don't care if it is the Surgeon General of the United States. Understood?

"Yes, sir."

"I want that..." *Miss Avery unapproved choice of words*, "...phone records, text, email, everything you can get on him sooner than you can get them."

"Yes, sir."

"Riley?"

"Yes, sir?"

I expected to witness a remarkable ripping at this point. I was surprised.

"Momma and baby, OK?"

"Real well, sir. She's gonna break a lot of hearts."

Stopping and turning to Riley, Stavlo said, "We'll teach her how to do it and not get caught in the act."

Riley smiled.

"Get the ball rolling on these items, then go home to them. Need you fresh tomorrow."

"Yes, sir."

He turned to me on the way back down, disappointment written across his face.

"What?"

"We missed it?"

"What?

"Desert." He looked at me as though I were significantly slower than Riley having a bad day. "Damn. Molly makes the best deserts."

"Seriously."

"You've never had her deserts. I hope she didn't go home."

The ride back to his place was almost as fast as the ride to the hospital.

"She's still here," he said, seeing her car as he pulled up.

There is crème brûlée and then there is Molly's crème brûlée.

There is a difference.

FRIDAY 10:42 A.M.

I moved through the morning somewhat in a daze. Even Rocket Scientist sensed something was wrong as he followed closely at my heels as I prepared. Mike also kept asking me how things were and if I was OK. On the way home the night before I had decided it best not to tell him about the events at the hospital. When I arrived at the church, it was blessedly empty, I went to work on redoing the bulletins so as not to embarrass Miss Avery again and preparing for Canon Bob's visit. Stavlo had promised he would be here for that.

The phone rang several times, but each time it didn't look important, so I let it go. After a while, I stopped looking at the caller ID and only noticed the light flashing an hour or so after the last call.

"If you're trying to sell me tickets to a Brewer's game, I'm going to be very disappointed," I said as I entered the code for the voicemail.

"You have two new message, received today...."

"Oh, for the the love of Pete."

Patience.

"First Message: Padre. We got Elvis. Keeps talking about a red demon coming out of the church. He's terrified that we can't protect him...." *Language.* "...Does that mean anything to you? Said he could identify the demon if we need him to...." *Language, Detective!* "...I'll be in touch." There was a brief pause, "And for cryin' out loud, get a cellphone. To delete this mess...."

I pressed 2 to save it. It would be funny when all this was over.

"Next message: Hi Father. It's Janine. When you have a

minute, please give me a call. I don't think its really important, but thanks. Bye."

Important or not, I called her back immediately. The operator patched me through to her room and she answered on the first ring.

"Hello."

"Janine? Hi, it's Father Anthony."

"Hi, Father. How are you?"

"A bit worn out from all the excitement, but doing OK? More importantly, how are you?"

"Mom had to run home for awhile, so it's quiet. There's still plenty of police around though."

"I somehow suspect that they'll be there for the duration."

"I still don't understand."

"I'm not sure anyone does."

I waited, but she was silent.

"You had something you wanted to discuss? Would you like for me to come down?"

"Oh, no. Sorry. Just drifted there for a minute."

"Understandable."

"I keep thinking about the night that the Dean was murdered. I keep running through the details."

"You need to rest," I said, thinking she was fretting over things that couldn't be changed.

"I am," she said reassuringly, "and it has helped me remember something."

"What's that?"

"Well, it's more a question and I thought maybe the answer would help me remember more."

"OK."

"Did Jimmy see anything that night?"

"Jimmy?"

"Yeah."

"Janine, he wasn't in that evening. He wasn't planning to come in until Saturday, after the Bishop's funeral."

"Oh... but he was there."

"Oh?"

"As I was running through the cloister. I know it was him I saw going downstairs to the classrooms. Well...," she said uncertainly, "I thought it was him, but it was pretty quick. I only saw his back as he made the corner heading downstairs. It's still so messed up," she said, now clearly doubting herself. "If he had been there he would have said something. Right?"

"Most certainly."

"Yeah."

"But you did see someone else that night? Someone going downstairs," I asked.

"No doubt," she answered.

"We need to let Detective Stavlo know. I'll give him a call, if that's OK. He'll probably want to stop by and ask you a few questions."

"Not a problem. I'll call off Mom." I could hear her smile.

"OK. Anything else?"

"No. Not right now."

We hung up, but I didn't call Stavlo immediately.

Junior detectives can sometimes be idiots.

I sat at my desk trying to figure out who else could have been there that night.

"Could have been anyone," I said, as I wandered the halls.

I turned right out of the offices and right down the west cloister. Turning right again I walked through the pass way between the west and east cloister and between the offices and St. Mary's Courtyard. I stopped at the stairs leading down to the classrooms.

"Who did she see?"

Turning on the lights I went downstairs and walked through each classroom, turning on the lights in each classroom as I went, but not turning them off. The only room that I had not looked was the custodian's closet.

"This is ridiculous," I said, opening the door and peering in.

A pull chain turned on the bare 60 watt bulb that didn't quite pierce every shadow.

"What?" I asked the mops, brooms and other cleaning supplies. "What?"

There was nothing more than what I had expected. Cleaning supplies, paper products, extra mop heads. Tucked in between the glass cleaner and the furniture polish was a folded piece of construction paper. Out of nothing but curiosity, I pulled it out. It was a child's drawing, probably something that had fallen off the wall or a note from one of the children to Jimmy...

Up until then, I thought it only happened in the movies, but I experienced how slow motion can happen in real life.

As I opened the drawing, several sheets of paper fell out. When I bent to retrieve them, already deciding that I was being nosey and just needed to put it back, I saw that what had fallen out were checks, covered in blood, and made out to the 'Emerging Artists' Consortium.' They were dated the same date as the bishop's funeral.

It took me several moments to understand, but when it registered, it was all I could do not to be sick. It rose up in my stomach as the thoughts and possibilities came crashing into my head.

I turned and walked back toward the stairs. My mind was frozen. Not comprehending.

"Father?"

Someone called from down the hall.

"Father?"

I looked up.

"Jimmy."

I looked down again at the checks. Still not comprehending, but then, like the waves of the Red Sea crashing down on the Egyptian army, I did not understand why, but I knew who. I looked up and the guilt and contempt in his eyes was all the confession necessary.

"Jimmy." As the name crossed my lips, it was not a question or a call. It was an accusation and a declaration of guilt.

His posture and eyes indicated that he understood it to be the same.

Like an old western, we stood staring at one another, waiting for the other to make the first move. I had less practice. I broke for the stairs. He was several steps behind me and actually lagging behind, even though I ran like a three towed sloth with two toes. He had not fully recovered from his injuries and that was to my advantage.

I entered the pass through hallway and went left. When I hit the west cloister I should have gone left again, but went right instead, toward the sanctuary. I heard him not far behind.

I like horror movies, even the B-rated horror movies. Don't know why, but even the goofy Elvira Mistress of the Dark Saturday afternoon movie marathons can cause me to fall behind in my work. As the sad people in these sad movies are being slaughtered for their stupidity, Zekey Boy and I will watch and maintain a running commentary on how easily they could have escaped if they had only done "X", and when they don't do "X" we berate them to no end and fully discern that they deserved the fate that the machete wielding maniac dealt out. Hence, when it came to me being chased through the hallways of St. Matthew's Church, Z-Man would have buried his face in utter shame.

Instead of running outdoors for all I was worth, I turned left into the sanctuary and immediately left again into the under-passage doorway, closed it behind me, intending to run through the under-passage only to discover that some idiot had locked the damn door.

"Who the bloody...," then I remembered, the idiot was me. The kids had been creeping through this past Sunday, so, after the recessional hymn I had locked it behind me to keep them at bay. It had worked, but now, as I kept my foot against the entry door to keep Jimmy out, I had no where else to go, but up. Another classic idiotic mistake of every horror movie.

Who goes up, my mind asked. *Only those who end up dead, you dip....*

"Shut up."

Jimmy slammed against the other side of the door.

"C'mon, Tony. We can talk this out. Settle it. It'll make sense, just let me in!" The last word was emphasized with another crash to the door.

I knew there would be no talking. The third slam against the door popped the top hinge and the door leaned in on me. No more time. I took a deep breath, placed my other foot on the step leading up....

"Hail Mary, full of grace...."

... and ran.

It was a five story jump from the top of the tower onto steps or sidewalks below. I might could make it onto the slate roof of the church, but that would either send me through into the sanctuary or sliding down to the same end. I thought of holding the door closed, but it opened in instead of out. After one more acrophobic look over the edge, I turned. Jimmy was standing in the doorway, winded, but otherwise looking just fine. For every hour I had spent growing soft behind my desk, he had spent in physical labor. He wasn't one of those beefy guys, but there would be no match.

"Tony. Tony. Tony," he said, a sneer on his face. "Don't mind if I call you Tony, do ya? All that 'Father this' and 'Father that' has soured my gut for over a decade."

I looked around one more time for a way out, but there was none except through him. He understood what I was thinking.

"Oh, Tony, you'll get down from here just fine. It'll be a lot quicker than the way you got up, but you'll be down in a jiffy," he said, coming toward me without hesitation.

"Wait," I said, backing up to the low stone wall that made up the perimeter of the tower. If I wasn't careful I would pitch myself over the edge.

"Wait for what," he asked, but stopped his advance just the same.

"Jimmy, what is this all about? Why? If I'm going to die, I'd at least like to know why. Why did you kill Dean Harris?"

A WEEK AGO THIS PAST FRIDAY

Jimmy entered through the north porch of the sanctuary, knowing that everyone would be down in the Parish Hall, it was easy enough to hide in should someone come wandering through. After taking a peek through the swinging doors leading in from the entry hall, he strolled on in, confident that he would be undisturbed; however, once inside, he stood still, listening for anyone who might be praying in the dark.

"Not even a church mouse," he said, moving toward the front of the church and the sacristy doors. Once there, he pulled the retractable chord that was attached to his belt with the key ring on the end and quickly found the key to the sacristy. He had used it many times before. In fact, for over a decade he had used this same set of keys to let himself in anywhere in the building he chose. If they only knew... except now, one of them did.

It was less than a year ago that the Dean had caught him.

"With my hand in the cookie jar," he said, as he unlocked the door.

But his confidence was back now. Had been for several months. He had gotten away with this for over a decade and he figured it would be another decade before they would even come close to catching him again, but he knew he wasn't planning to make the same mistake twice. He had become over confident. He had let his guard down. He had let that priest sneak up on him.

"And that's what he had done. He snuck up on me like he

didn't trust me. After all this time I've been cleaning their toilets and scraping the gum off the floors from when they brats spit it out instead of putting it in the trash bin."

He said all this to himself as he quickly turned the dial on the safe in the sacristy. Stupid fools kept it on a sticky note stuck on the inside of one of the cabinets, but he didn't need to look, having memorized it years ago. He still couldn't believe that the Dean had not changed the combination after catching him, but that just made it easier and proved to him how stupid these folks really were.

He turned the dial and then pushed the lever down.

"As easy as falling off a greased log," he said to himself as he swung the door open. "Oh, Mrs. Nancy, you're going to be happy with this month's bonus."

The collection from the Bishop's funeral, which was to be given to some weird charity, was...

"My cup runneth over," Jimmy said, pulling out the plates.

He was careful not to take all the large bills. A few $100s, plenty of $50s, and enough Andrew Jacksons to keep the slots dinging for a month. He had figured it would be a good day, but had never planned on this. He began shoving the cash in his pockets as quickly as a kid shoves candy into his Jack-o-lantern when he finds an unattended stash on the front porch of an absent neighbor.

Feeling his bulging pockets, he had decided that he had enough, too much more and someone would notice...

"Except for you," he said, snatching one more $100 out of the plates.

... when the lights came on.

He didn't move, he didn't turn, only trying to hide what he was up to.

"Just cleaning up," he said, over his shoulder, not noticing who it was. "Be out in a few."

"We've talked about this before, Jimmy."

Damnit.

"Dean Harris, sir. Honestly," he said, turning to face the Dean, knocking some of the cash and checks to the floor, "I came in here and found this all open. Wasn't me. I swear."

"Did you know, Jimmy," the Dean said, walking in and past him without looking at him. "following each service, the ushers count the offering, fill out a receipt and place it in an envelope, and then place that envelope under the treasurer's door? Only after they have counted everything, do they put it back in the plates."

The Dean turned and faced him.

"No."

"Did you also know that just this past year, we discovered a discrepancy.. an error between the amount counted and the amount deposited and that this amount exceeded $200,000?"

"I never stole that much," Jimmy said, himself shocked at the amount.

"No, I don't suppose you did. I'm willing to admit that some accounting errors probably occurred, my fault for allowing it to continue, but I would be willing to wager it all that a vast majority of that money ended up in your pocket."

Jimmy was silent.

"The last time I caught you in here, I made it clear, if you were caught again, I would report it. Based on what I can see spilling out of your pockets, the amount you've taken this time is substantial."

"Well," Jimmy said, finding his voice, and a sarcastic one at that, "the amount you took in today was *substantial*."

"This is not acceptable," the Dean said, moving to walk past Jimmy.

"Ask me if I care."

They looked into each others eyes and the Dean must have understood that this may end differently than before. Turning quickly, he went to the small entrance of the sacristy that lead directly onto the altar area, slapping the row of switches and turning on the lights as he went. Jimmy quickly ducked out the other sacristy door and met him on the other side.

"Jimmy."

"Dean."

Jimmy walked up the steps onto the altar area. He was trapped and he moved like it, but in his mind, he was not caught. Not yet.

"Jimmy, I told you then that I would provide you with whatever you needed. If you needed financial assistance, if you needed a raise, if you needed a loan, I was prepared to help you, but it came with a condition. Do you remember the condition?"

Silence.

"Thou shall not steal."

"Don't preach at me, preacher man," he said, spitting the words out.

"I'm not preaching, Jimmy. I'm only reminding."

"Well, I don't need no reminding either."

"Jimmy, take what's in your pockets and go home, but don't come back. I'm letting you go. File for unemployment, do whatever you need to do, but you are not to show yourself around here again."

Whether it was pride or just pure meanness, something welled up inside Jimmy. He wasn't going anywhere.

"And why would I want to give up such easy money," he said, pulling out a wad of cash from his pocket and shaking it, careful to not let a single bill slip free.

"Because that," the Dean said, pointing at Jimmy's cash engorged clenched fist, "belongs to God and His church. That is for the Kingdom!"

"No, Dean Harris," he yelled, "this is not for the *Kingdom*, it was printed in the bulletin, its for the Emerging Artists' Consortium! What the hell has that got to do with the *Kingdom*?"

The Dean bowed his head and ran his hand over the top of his head and through his hair.

"I don't know."

"Exactly," Jimmy said, leaning forward, thinking he had won the argument. "So why do you care? Why do you care if I have it or the damn emerging artist have it!"

"Because, Jimmy," the Dean said, looking up and more calm than Jimmy thought possible, "'Thou shall not steal.' Don't you see? I personally don't give two hoots about the emerging artist and I don't care about the money, we have enough, but what I do care about is you. I care about your soul. I care about what stealing from this church, or anybody else for that matter, is doing to you. Jimmy, this isn't about things temporal, temporary, this is about things eternal, and I think you need... saving."

Jimmy wasn't a great thinker or philosopher. He wasn't a great church goer either. Occasionally he would show up at one of the local churches, but that was more for looks than faith. Neither was he one who thought about things temporal or eternal. Jimmy was about satisfying his immediate need and Jimmy was about satisfying whatever itch Nancy might have and keeping her off his back so that he could sit down down on a Sunday afternoon and watch the games on his big screen. So, when the Dean started talking about needing to be saved, he knew the conversation was lost. He knew that he was either going to walk the path that the Dean was hoping to place him on or he was going to walk the path that put him comfortably on his couch.

The couch won.

He turned as though in thought, and he was, but it was about how to finish this conversation. And there they were: a relic and a hammer, they would do nicely.

He took a few steps away from the Dean and across the altar area. Reaching out, he picked up the paver and the fistula.

"Dean. Dean," he said, taking several steps backwards, "I just don't know what to do."

"Jimmy...."

Had Jimmy known, he would have heard his name spoken as a prayer, instead, he heard it as a condemnation.

The paver caught the Dean on the temple, but only his head snapped to the side. He stood firmly in place. Jimmy yelled.

Janine heard.

Jimmy shoved the Dean, not really knowing that the Dean's heart was already shattering itself.

The Dean fell into the cathedra, a seat he had envied and aspired to all his ordained career, but one he knew he would never be granted, and in the end, one his soul knew he never wanted.

The Dean's eyes pleaded, but Jimmy did not listen.

He stabbed the fistula into the Dean's chest, but it didn't even pierce the fabric of his shirt. So, using the paver, he hammered. He hammered until at least eight inches of the piping had entered the Dean's chest. The blood pumped out like water from the city park fountain.

Dean Harris, although Episcopalian, had always cherished the Latin words of that most cleansing rite.

"*Ego te absolv...,*" he whispered, but was only able to finish the absolution in his dying heart.

Jimmy, on the other hand, had no idea what it meant, thinking the Dean was cursing him. He had to move.

"Go," he said to himself. And he did.

Avoiding the pool of blood on the white marble floor, he ran down the steps and back up into the sacristy. He reached down and grabbed the checks that had fallen to the floor, smearing them in blood.

"Well that's not going to come out," he said, and shoved everything into his pocket.

He washed the blood from his hand in that little sink, what did they call it? A pissina? They had told him that it was not to be used under any circumstances.

"Why have a sink if you can't use it?" He asked those reminders in his head as he scrubbed the blood from his hands. Had he looked in a mirror, his own bloody reflection would have given him a fright. He then pulled out a cleaning rag that he had tucked away in one of the closets and quickly wiped the offering plates and safe. His fingerprints were all over the church, but he thought it best if they didn't appear on the cookie jar.

"Dean Harris," a woman called from the back of the sanctuary and almost caused him to mess his shorts.

He froze. They were coming.

"Dean Harris." Closer.

He moved quickly, putting the offering plates back into the safe, closing it, and spinning the dial. As he was closing the cabinet: "Dean Harris? Oh, my God."

Running.

"Dean, what happened?"

Jimmy picked up the paver, he thought he might just need it again before this was over with, walked to the entrance of the sacristy and peered around the corner. He couldn't see who it was and he didn't think they would see him either in the darkness of the nave. He started walking up the far aisle.

"Dean. Dean Harris."

Jimmy stopped.

"Oh, God."

Jimmy started moving again, but the board under his foot gave a loud creak.

"Who's there? Hello?

Ducking down behind the pew, Jimmy cursed himself. He knew this place. Every inch of it and he knew that board creaked every damn time someone stepped on it.

He didn't dare look up for fear of being seen, but as he listened he heard them go into the sacristy. He looked. He knew her immediately, even at a distance, because he had been admiring her figure for quite awhile. Janine Kline. When she had her back to him, he quickly moved again to the recess of the north porch entry. He backed into the shadows to watch, but no sooner had he hidden himself than the upstart came in from the west cloister entrance. Had he bothered to look up, he would have clearly seen Jimmy staring across the pews at him.

Why was he whistling? What an idiot, Jimmy thought. Looking up the aisle, he had direct line of sight into the sacristy, he saw that Janine had also heard the whistling.

"Excuse me, sir," the upstart called.

Watching, Jimmy fully expected Janine to come running out, but instead, she froze for a moment, then turned toward the back of the sacristy. Something caught her eye and she picked is up then made her way quietly through the under-passage door.

"Now why would you do that?" Jimmy whispered.

"Sir!"

Upstart still hadn't figured out what was what. Jimmy watched as Tony approached the Dean.

"Shi...."

Tony slipped and hit the floor hard. A bark of laughter escaped Jimmy's lips and he clapped his hands over his mouth. He waited. The upstart wasn't moving.

"Hope you appreciate the shine I put on that floor, boy," Jimmy said, as he saw his opportunity to escape. He was nearly to the staff parking lot entrance when he remembered he still had all the checks. That stupid rock was going in the Menomonee, but the checks were a different matter. He couldn't afford to be caught with them and Nancy would be furious if he kept them. Early on he had brought checks home thinking he could figure out how to cash them, but Nancy had given him such grief that he didn't dare do it again, especially with everything else that had gone wrong.

Thinking as quickly as he could, he doubled back and headed to the stairs leading down to the classrooms. He then heard a door slam.

"Under passage."

It was followed by someone running in his direction. He thought it was the Kline woman. He made it to the corner of the stairwell and out of sight, certain that she hadn't seen him.

Her steps faded as she continued down the west cloister, but someone chasing her made the turn into the crossway. Jimmy watched from the shadows as Tony ran by and then heard him hit the crash bar of the east cloister doors.

"Damnit!"

"Some holy man you are," Jimmy whispered, making his

way down the stairs and to the utility closet.

On the way, he snatched some brat's scribbles off the wall, stuffed the bloody checks into it, and put it up on the shelf. He wasn't at all concerned about someone finding it.

"No one ever looks in here. Not a damn one of them would know a dust mop if it reached out and slapped them in the face," he said, with another bark of laughter.

As he made his way back up the stairs he heard Tony running back toward the sanctuary. He smiled to himself and walked calmly out the staff parking lot doors, making sure they didn't bang behind him, and then he ran.

FRIDAY 10:53 A.M.

"Why?" Jimmy asked, pushing his hair back. "Let's just say I've exceeded the limit for this to be a petty crime."

"But Jimmy... the Dean. This is a church." I don't know why I thought that would make any difference to a person who had no problem with murdering a priest. Somewhere in my mind, it still meant something. It didn't to Jimmy.

"You all ain't no church," he yelled. "This place is a rich kids' club and you and Dean is nothing more than the club presidents. Walkin' around in your fancy clothes acting like you was a king or something."

"That's not true, Jimmy." I wasn't cynical enough to believe it.

"I've seen the finance reports for this place. You all got more money than Rockefeller, but you pay someone to clean your toilets as little as possible. And you let them work as little as possible so that you don't have to dish out any extra. You got all that fine silver that you bring out once a week and show off, then you shove it back in the vault once it's all polished up again."

"Jimmy, some things are holy. They're sacred. They're intended to honor God."

"Oh, hells bells." Disgusted. "You honor God while there are hundreds around you suffering. Well, I'll tell you what, I got my share," he said, stabbing himself in the chest with his finger. "Nancy and me got our share of your pie and we ain't about to give it back or give it up. Dean got in the way and he paid. You got in the way, now you gonna pay."

He moved forward. There was nowhere to go.

"Jimmy!" One last time to stall him.

"What?"

"But why Miss Avery, Jimmy? Why her?"

"Well, now, I do feel bad about that," he said, stepping back. "She's one ya'll gonna force to work until she's dead."

I shook my head.

"That little hot number, Janine," he continued, "well it finally struck me what she took that night in the sacristy. The Dean's little book that he keeps all his secrets in. You know he wrote down all these things that he could hold over people, so as to force them to do his will. I know he had stuff on me in there and I figured that's why she took it, had stuff on her too," he shook his head in amazement. "Can't believe she went in with Leigh."

"You knew about them?"

"You see, that's ya'lls problem. To you, I'm just Jimmy. Jimmy, there's a stain on the carpet. Jimmy, there's a leak in the kitchen. Jimmy, 'Clean up on aisle four,'" he said, making his hands into a megaphone. "You say it and you know I'll head right over. You know I'll clean up your messes, but until you actually need me to do something," he shook his head, "you don't see me, so I walk through this place like a ghost... until some little brat misses the toilet and you need someone to clean it up!

"Of course I knew about them," waving it off. "When they thought no one was around, they was always *clandestinely* touching one another. They just didn't know ol' Jimmy was watchin', but I figured the Dean seen 'em too. He was always watchin'.

"Well, I didn't give two hoots about what he wrote about her in that book of his, but I didn't need anyone reading up on me. When the police didn't come looking for me that first day I figured they hadn't found it, so Nancy and me figured it was in his office. We went in early that morning to find it, but we spent too much time looking and poor Miss A. came in." Shooing his guilt away like a bothersome gnat, he added, "She's a tough ol' bird. She's fine."

"But who hit you?"

"You don't listen so good, do ya' Tony?"

"Perhaps not, but I do."

The voice startled us so badly that we both nearly went over the edge.

"You Ok there, Padre?"

The cavalry has arrived!

"Looks like I might live after all," I said to Stavlo, as he casually walked onto the roof. He positioned himself to the side of Jimmy and I, then reached into his vest and pulled out a pair of handcuffs. He played with them absentmindedly as he spoke, never once taking his eyes from Jimmy.

"It was Nancy, Padre, who clouted Jimmy. They had a little covering up to do. I'm guessing they were moments away from being seen my Miss Avery, so he hit her a good one from behind. Coward's way, really. Little ol' lady like that." Shook his head. "But when they didn't find the Dean's little black book, a lightbulb went off in Jimmy's head. You said you saw Janine pick something up that night and you figured it was that little black book."

Jimmy was silent, but he was also looking for a way out.

"By the way, we caught your little errand boy last night, Jimmy. Fred Riner. Ring a bell."

"Never heard of him," Jimmy said, a bit too quickly.

"That's OK. He's already IDed Nancy. Several nice police personnel are on their way to pick her up. Padre," he said, still not taking his eyes off Jimmy, "Jimmy here did some interior painting for Janine. She paid him twice what anyone else would have gotten, because she liked him. She also trusted him, so she gave him a key to her place so that he could come and go as he needed. By then, Jimmy had already made a pretty good living out of stealing, so just in case he thought he might want to take another look see in Janine's place, he made a spare for himself.

"Mr. Riner says that he doesn't off anyone without knowing the reason, calls it insurance in the event his employer forgets to pay. Mr. Riner informed us just a short while ago - he's being very helpful, don'tcha know - that you told him about that little black book, what it contained, and that you and Nancy couldn't afford for anyone, including Janine, knowing its content. That reason and your $1,500 was good enough for him.

"I'll tell you what I find funny, though, Padre: Nancy whacked Jimmy such a good one that one more foot pound per square inch of force just might have caved Jimmy's dumb ol' skull in for good."

Jimmy's face darkened, but he was still silent. Still thinking.

"Bet you two had a pretty good row over that one, didn't you, Jimmy."

Jimmy responded.

"Language, Jimmy," Stavlo said, gleefully. "Padre and I have been working on ours and after that little outburst I would definitely say that you need to do the same. Miss Avery would not approve."

Jimmy responded again.

Seeing that he had finally gotten a rise out of Jimmy, Stavlo turned his attention to me, but his eyes remained on Jimmy.

"Padre?"

"Yes, sir."

"You won't die of radiation poisoning! Get a cellphone, ya luddite!"

"Yes, sir."

"I was already on my way here, but it would have saved me a maniacs drive the last few miles if I had been able to reach you."

"Why the last few miles?"

"That's when Janine called me. Said you were supposed to be calling and wanted to make sure that you had."

"Ah."

"Padre?"

"Yes, sir."

"You should've called."

Junior detective may be losing his badge.

"Yes, sir."

"Jimmy, I'm sick of looking at you. Let's go," he said, waving Jimmy to come to him.

Jimmy ignored and walked over to the edge.

"Jimmy, don't," I said. "Trust me, I already thought about it."

Stavlo didn't move.

After a few more seconds of desperate thought, Jimmy hung his head.

"That's what I thought," Stavlo said, walking over to him and taking a firm grip on his arm.

Jimmy tried to yank free, but Stavlo put a little Chuck Norris on him and Jimmy found himself face down on the roof with a knee planted not so gently into his back.

"James Owens, you have the right to remain silent...," Stavlo began as he placed the cuffs on Jimmy. Once complete, he heaved Jimmy to his feet and began marching him toward the door leading down.

"Come on, Padre. I know it's still morning, but let's drop this sack of... let's drop this coward off with some fine individuals in blue and go get a beer. What do you say?"

I didn't know what to say, but it sounded like a fine idea to me. I followed, looking back only once, considering what might have happened.

I looked up.

"They didn't teach us this sort of thing in seminary, you know."

God chuckled.

The Bible is full of stories of betrayal, you just never think they apply to you.

After Jimmy had been deposited in the back of a squad car, Stavlo let Riley know where we would be. Ten minutes later we were sitting in the back of a quiet pub having a beer. Well, he was having a beer and I was having a beer if you can call twelve-year-old scotch a beer.

"I still don't understand," I said, shaking my head. "Could he really have taken that much?"

"Hank Slidell came in this morning. That $200,000 or so that was missing...."

"Yeah."

"Hank tells me that following each service the ushers bring the offering, count it out, and complete a form. They then put the offering back in the plate and the form they put in the Treasurer's box in the office."

"Yeah. It's a check and balance system we have."

"That's good, but in order for a check and balance system to work, someone's got to follow through on the checking and the balancing. Apparently the former treasurers never did. They always trusted and assumed everything was kosher. Those little forms, hundreds of them, had just been dropped into a file without a second look. Hank came on board and gave them a second look. There were some addition errors along the way, but Jimmy and Nancy probably got away with close to that $200,000."

"That's incredible."

"Yes, it is. You said earlier that the Chapter voted to write it off without investigating."

"Surely, after catching Jimmy in the past, the Dean would have put two and two together."

"We'll never know for sure. I'm guessing he worked it out, but for some reason decided not to say anything."

"He was probably trying to help him and keep him out of trouble." I couldn't believe it. "Jimmy said that no one saw him, but the Dean saw him, loved him, and forgave him, even of something so great."

"Better man than me."

Double-D, I looked at my soul in shame, remembering what I had thought of him when he was alive. *I pray you'll forgive me for thinking so poorly of you. I pray you are now able to rest in peace.*

"And someone else saw him leaving the church on the night of the Dean's murder."

"Really! Who?"

"Elvis."

"Elvis?"

"Yep. We picked him up yesterday evening as he was hunting for some food. He kept going on about the Red Demon, terrified that there weren't enough po-lice to keep him safe. I'm guessing that Jimmy boy didn't know his face was covered in the Dean's blood, so when he come running out, Elvis thought he was seeing...."

"A Red Demon."

"Yep. I asked him if he could recognize that particular demon again and he assured me he could. Jimmy and Nancy got away with their activity for a decade, but no more. If I have my way, neither will see another free day in their lives."

My heart found that sad.

"Jimmy...." I could think of nothing more to say.

We sat in silence for a long time and when the waitress brought us another round, we chinked our glasses and went back to our own thoughts.

A half hour had past, when a not so funny funny thought hit me.

"Hum."

"What's that?"

"I think we've got six out of the seven deadly sins covered."

"That so?"

"Lust, greed, sloth, anger, envy, and pride."

"Sloth? Really? Seems everyone's been pretty busy to me," Stavlo said.

"I always think of the church when it comes to that one. A spiritual laziness. We should have seen this. And Jimmy is right on one point."

"Do tell."

"We never really saw him. We never really see a lot of

folks who are on the periphery. Who aren't our *kind*."

"Please don't justify his actions. He was a thief and a murderer."

"No. Not justifying him at all. Just saying we as the church need to do better."

He nodded and the silence returned for awhile.

"That was only six."

"Six what?"

"Six of the seven deadly sins. I'm gonna cut you off if you start forgetting too much."

"Ah," I said, sliding my drink out of his reach. "Gluttony. I couldn't fit in gluttony."

"Oh, I can," he said, pointing toward the door of the pub.

Canon Bob came waddling in.

I couldn't swallow fast enough and spewed my drink across the table.

That set Stavlo off laughing and he couldn't force himself to stop, even after Canon Bob stood looming over us, beefy hands on hips.

"We had a two o'clock meeting," he barked, looking at us with annoyance, "and I find you both here drinking!"

"Bob," I said without the slightest fear of repercussion, "I would gladly serve at St. Swithin's in the Swamp if it got me away from the madness I've experienced these last two weeks. Pull up a chair and join us."

"Don't be absurd."

Stavlo's laughter ceased abruptly. "Bob, have a seat."

Bob surprised himself by sitting quickly.

This guy really could come in handy.

"Bob, let this nice lady bring you a drink and we'll tell you about the case of the golden fistula. It's a good one. You'll like it. April," he said, turning to the waitress who had kindly wiped up my mess, "bring Bob a beer."

"Make it a sherry, please. It's way too early for something as crass as beer."

That started Stavlo in again on the laughter. I tried to

control myself, but was unsuccessful. After a moment, even though he had no idea why, Canon Bob joined in. It was a full on riot and some of the tension of these last few weeks was beginning to pass.

When the waitress... when April - *I am going to start 'seeing' everyone as best I can* - set Canon Bob's drink in front of him, Stavlo and I began telling our story. It was late afternoon before the three of us stood to leave. We had had a good lunch and switched to coffee and tea a few hours before.

Turns out Canon Bob wasn't such a bad guy after all and maybe, just maybe, I had exorcised some of the bad egg from my own soul. As for Stavlo. Well...

EPILOGUE: ELEVEN MONTHS LATER

The Fifth Column met in the back room of a small church on the outskirts of the city. There was no fear of being caught, as this was one of the many churches that had closed over the course of the last several years due to the ineptitude of the former Bishop and the general apostate direction the national church had taken over the course of the last several years.

This emergency meeting had been called following the announcement of the slate of clergy up for election as the next Diocesan Bishop. In their opinion, every candidate would bring about further decay of God's one holy catholic and apostolic church, which would lead to its ultimate collapse.

They could have done what so many others had done, abandon the church, taken their marbles and gone home, but unlike those others, these were not spineless. They were the Fifth Column and they refused to turn over the keys to the Church - or at least this Diocese - to Satan and the reprobate.

"If anyone of these is elected, it'll be chaos, but if she is elected... it will fall."

"Then we must see to it that she is not elected."

"How then do you plan to stop it? A smear campaign of sorts?"

"Oh, my brother, I think we are a long ways past smear campaigns. That'll only inflame her legion."

"What are you suggesting we do then?"

"St. Peter carried a sword and was not afraid to use it when necessary."

Silence.

"What am I suggesting? I am suggesting the time is nigh."

Made in the USA
Lexington, KY
08 November 2019